NURSE ON TRIAL

D0417291

Paula Garland is shattered after she fails her SRN because of a traumatic experience in her final year, so when she is given a second chance to sit her exams she resolves to put the past behind her. Then she meets Dr Justin Stewart and it seems as if history will repeat itself . . .

NURSE ON TRIAL

BY

CLARE LAVENHAM

MILLS & BOON LIMITED
London · Sydney · Toronto

First published in Great Britain 1982
by Mills & Boon Limited, 15–16 Brook's Mews,
London W1A 1DR

ISBN 0 263 74024 2

Set in 11 on 12½ pt Linotron Times

03/0982

Photoset by Rowland Phototypesetting Ltd
Bury St Edmunds, Suffolk
Made and printed in Great Britain by
Richard Clay (The Chaucer Press) Ltd
Bungay, Suffolk

CHAPTER ONE

EVEN now, although twenty-four hours had gone by, Paula had scarcely begun to come to terms with it. She stood at her window in the Nurses' Home, staring out at the spires and tower blocks of London but seeing nothing of the familiar view, thinking only of yesterday's bitter disappointment.

It had all been useless—that frantic period of block study, the total exclusion of social life, the desperate last-minute revision. Nothing had been any good. She had failed.

Behind her there was a tap on the door and a tall girl with long pale hair came in. She was wearing cord trousers and a blue shirt and carried an outsize handbag.

Paula turned round reluctantly. She didn't want to see anyone just then, least of all Mary Shipton who had been in her set right through the hospital and had now crowned a very successful three years by winning the gold medal.

'I thought you were leaving early,' she said ungraciously.

'I'm just off.' Mary glanced round the room. 'Haven't you even started to pack?'

'There's plenty of time. I'm only going home, not catching a plane to—where is it?'

'Corfu. I'm meeting the rest of the party at Gatwick and my taxi's due in a few minutes. I did most of my packing last night so I'm all organised.'

She would be, Paula thought sourly. Mary was always well organised. Even her revising for the exam had been orderly, leaving her brain cool and clear for tackling the questions. No wonder she had done so well.

'Do you know which ward you'll be sent to when you come back?' Paula asked. 'I know you're going to be a staff nurse at West City, of course, but—'

'They haven't got us all sorted out yet. I shall have to wait until I come back from holiday. Er—I suppose you haven't heard what's happening to yourself yet?'

'I'm seeing Miss Grieves this morning. In about ten minutes, actually.'

'So that's why you're looking so neat and smart.'

Paula glanced down at the cream suit which she had worn at her sister's wedding last year. Although it was too conventional for her taste, she was obliged to admit it looked good with her golden brown hair, and the emerald shirt she wore with it brightened the green of her eyes.

Apart from a slight pallor—which made the freckles on her nose stand out more than usual—she showed no sign of the strain she had been under or the appalling shock she had received when the exam results were published.

'I must be off.' Mary hesitated, looking a little

awkward. 'Don't worry too much, Paula. I'm sure they'll let you stay on—if that's what you want.'

Paula wasn't sure what she wanted but she had no intention of saying so. Mary would be shocked if she admitted she was tempted to make a quick getaway so that she could begin as soon as possible on the enormous task of forgetting three wasted years.

'I shall have to see what Miss Grieves says.' She looked at her watch. 'Goodbye, Mary. I hope you have a super time in Corfu.'

As soon as the other girl had gone she started out on the long walk to the administrative offices in West City's central block.

Under normal circumstances she would have gone by the subway, to emerge in the main hospital and thread her way through a maze of corridors to the entrance hall. But today she was strangely reluctant to take the well-known route. It was almost as though mentally she was already divorced from the hospital. Instead she chose the open air, crossing the narrow road which separated the Nurses' Home from the other buildings, passing the tiny garden and eventually coming to the courtyard before the pillared main door.

Leaving the sunshine behind her, she went up the few steps and entered the cool, antiseptic-smelling atmosphere of the vestibule.

She had walked quietly and sedately, yet her heart was thudding as she took a seat in the anteroom and waited to be summoned to the presence of the Principal Nursing Officer.

So much depended on the next few minutes. Her whole life perhaps.

There was a low murmur of voices from the inner room. Eventually a young nurse with flushed cheeks and tear-bright eyes came out, scurried past Paula and vanished. Almost immediately she heard her own name called.

There seemed to be an acre of pale grey carpet to be crossed before she reached the desk. She was vaguely aware of Adam-green walls and a lofty ceiling, one or two choice pictures and a beautiful arrangement of gladioli, but most of her attention was fixed on the woman sitting behind the desk.

She had only once or twice before spoken to the formidable Principal Nursing Officer and each time she had found her alarming. Massively built though not in the least fat, Miss Grieves was severely dressed in a perfectly tailored dark blue outfit with a small lace collar. Her grey hair looked as though the hairdresser had only just left it and her make-up had been applied with great artistry.

'Sit down, Nurse Garland.' She indicated a chair facing her but did not smile. 'There seems little point in pretending you don't know why I've sent for you.'

'No, Miss Grieves.' Paula's voice betrayed her tenseness.

'I'm sure you must be very disappointed with

your failure to pass your SRN exam—but perhaps not altogether surprised?'

'Not surprised? I'm sorry—I don't understand.'

There was a slight pause and then the Nursing Officer said quietly, 'I was under the impression that you've taken your nursing career rather lightly.'

Paula felt her colour deepening. She forgot to be nervous as she indignantly refuted the suggestion.

'Nursing meant a lot to me, Miss Grieves—it still does. I honestly don't think my attitude towards it was—was frivolous. I may have been a bit scatty at times but most student nurses are at the beginning.'

She was subjected to a long thoughtful stare and then Miss Grieves picked up a pile of papers and began to turn them over.

'I have here all the reports from your various ward sisters. I'm bound to tell you that most of them are critical of your general behaviour. The overall opinion seems to be that you have ability but don't always make the best use of it. At a time like this, when your future is being decided, these reports must be taken into account.'

Paula listened with a sinking heart. She sat staring down at her neatly folded hands and it seemed to her that the whole of the last three years unrolled before her like a film. Sister Graham would have given her a bad report, that was for sure, but she did the same to practically every young nurse, and Sister Walker had violently disapproved of any liaison between nurses and housemen. More than once she had caught Paula talking to a junior doctor in the kitchen.

It had been harmless enough, perhaps even a necessary loosening of tension, but Sister Walker had made a ridiculous fuss about it.

And the others? Paula couldn't think of anyone with whom she had not got on reasonably well.

'I'm afraid I was a bit silly in my first year,' she admitted, 'but I got over all that and settled down. I really worked terribly hard during the last few weeks.'

Too late she saw what a mistake it had been to say that.

Miss Grieves instantly pounced. 'The last few weeks, Nurse? I presume you mean you tried to make up for neglecting your studies in the past by frantic revision just before the exam. It never has paid dividends and it never will. Modern nursing is too vast a subject to be crammed into such a short time.'

Paula listened despairingly. It was all true— every word of it—and if she wanted to continue her defence she would have to mention the one subject she had wanted to steer clear of. Raising her eyes she looked straight across the desk into the grave face of the Nursing Officer.

'I passed through a very difficult period in my personal life about six months ago. For a while I couldn't study at all and by the time I'd recovered a little it was too late. The exam was almost on me.'

Miss Grieves nodded slightly and, to Paula's relief, did not ask her to elaborate. No doubt she already knew all about it. Once more she sat silently, her expression giving away nothing of her thoughts, and then she asked an abrupt question.

'What are your own feelings in this unfortunate matter? Do you want to continue with your nursing and sit state finals again?'

'Oh, Miss Grieves—' Hope flared into sudden life and unconsciously Paula straightened her drooping shoulders. 'Do you mean there's a chance for me? You're not going to turn me out?'

For the first time the Nursing Officer permitted herself a slight smile. 'Does it mean so much to you?'

Only a short while ago Paula had actually been wondering whether it wouldn't be a good idea to leave the hospital and make a fresh start. Now she knew with absolute certainty that it would break her heart to do so.

'Nursing is what I've always wanted to do,' she said simply.

'Then it's a pity you appear to have wasted your chances. However, now that I've spoken to you I'm prepared to give you another chance—'

'Oh, thank you—'

Miss Grieves held up her hand. 'One moment, Nurse. There are conditions attached which you may not care for. For one thing, you will have to wait another whole year before taking the exam. I don't intend to let you sit for it the next time it comes round. And for another, you will have to spend that year at our St Andrews Annexe at Belton Park. How do you feel about that?'

The dismayed face opposite was a clear indication of Paula's feelings. A whole year! It seemed an eternity. And at St Andrews too, six miles away on the outskirts of London, a one-time cottage hospital enlarged with huts during the Second World War and still not properly rebuilt.

'You've nursed there, I believe?' Miss Grieves asked.

'I was there for two months during my first year.'

'Then you will be familiar with it.' She folded her hands on the desk and leaned forward slightly. 'Those are my terms, Nurse, but you don't have to accept them. The choice is yours. Would you like a little time to think it over?'

Paula's hesitation was only slight. Instinctively she felt that to accept promptly would earn her a good mark and, besides, she wanted it settled. She couldn't bear the prospect of spending two weeks at home with her family unless she could tell them her future was no longer in jeopardy.

She said very clearly and steadily, 'No, thank you, Miss Grieves. I'd like to accept right now. I can't pretend I want to go and work at Belton Park, but I'll try to make the best of it.'

'Good.' This time the smile was warm and kindly. 'I must admit that is what I'd hoped you would say, but I must warn you that your general behaviour will be very closely watched. You will be, in a sense, on trial.'

'I quite understand,' Paula told her earnestly.

'You must remember that West City has no need to keep on girls who don't make the grade. Unlike the provincial hospitals we are never short of nurses. You've been very lucky to get another chance.'

'Yes, I know, Miss Grieves.' In response to a gesture of dismissal Paula stood up.

All the way back to her room she told herself how lucky she was and she repeated it many times during her two weeks holiday. Away from the inspiring presence of the Principal Nursing Officer it wasn't quite so easy to believe, particularly as her parents thought she had been treated far too severely.

'I don't know what Miss Grieves meant by your general behaviour being unsatisfactory,' her mother grumbled. 'It's a reflection on your upbringing.'

'She didn't mean it that way, only that I was too fond of fooling around when I should have been working, and I certainly didn't do enough studying.' Paula sighed. 'I shall probably have plenty of time for revision at St Andrews but I do wish I wasn't being exiled there, all the same.'

She wished it even more when the time came to

report for duty. In the taxi which took her there she thought back to her previous experience of the annexe. The Nurses' Home was small and cramped, and she had had to share a room with another girl. At eighteen she hadn't minded much but at twenty-one she viewed it differently, particularly under her present circumstances.

Fortunately the Home Warden, after welcoming her briskly, told her she had been allotted a small room on the ground floor, next to the fire escape door.

'I think you'll be able to squeeze yourself and your belongings into it.' She glanced at the suitcases and boxes. 'You seem to have brought everything except the kitchen sink.'

'I'm going to be here for a year,' Paula reminded her.

'Er—yes. It's very sensible of you to try and make your room seem like home, so long as you're prepared to keep it tidy.' The Warden unlocked a door at the end of a narrow corridor. 'I'll leave you to settle in, but stay around when you've finished because Miss Wallace will want to see you.'

Left alone, Paula looked round at the pale pink walls and fresh white paint, the old-fashioned dark oak furniture—which had obviously had a hard life—and thrust down the memory of her room at West City with its vanity unit, desk and angled lamp.

This wasn't at all bad really and it would look a

lot better when she had arranged her possessions the way she liked them. She worked hard for an hour and then surveyed her handiwork. The book-shelves were now full, with her text books well to the fore, and her toilet articles set out on the dressing-table; the shade on her bed lamp went well with the pink curtains and her pot plants seemed at home on the windowsill.

Satisfied, she sat down to await the summons to the office of the Senior Nursing Officer in charge at St Andrews. And then, quite suddenly, she noticed the silence.

The hospital was half-a-mile from the main road and surrounded by quiet residential streets. The hum of traffic—never ceasing at West City—was totally absent. There were no sounds of voices or footsteps or ambulance sirens. Nothing except the twitter of birds from the garden.

Paula sighed and looked at her watch. How on earth was she going to fill in the time before starting work in the morning? They didn't even have a canteen here, where she might have found some-one to talk to, and the hours stretched emptily ahead.

She was relieved as well as nervous when Miss Wallace sent for her.

The Senior Nursing Officer was a stranger who had only been in charge at St Andrews for a few months. Young, slim and very elegant in her dark dress, she had corn-coloured hair upswept in a neat roll and large grey eyes set amid skilfully darkened lashes. She received Paula coolly and at once got down to business.

'I'm putting you in the Intensive Care Unit, Nurse Garland. Have you had experience of that kind of nursing at West City?'

Forgetting to answer, Paula gazed at her in dismay. Any other ward she would have accepted with equanimity—but not the Unit, not after what had happened last Christmas. Dark painful memories crowded in on her, memories of another ICU at a hospital near her home.

'Did you hear the question, Nurse?' Miss Wallance enquired sharply.

'Oh—er—yes, thank you. I have worked in the ICU at West City but it was some time ago.'

'Then you'll remember that it's somewhat different from ordinary nursing and in some ways more exacting.'

'Yes, I do remember. Do I start on early duty in the morning?'

'I was coming to that.' The Nursing Officer picked up a list and glanced at it. 'I'm afraid I shall have to put you on night duty for the first week. It's not my policy to switch nurses around between day and night duty but at present I have several away on holiday and three off sick. It so happens that you'll be more needed at night for a short time.'

The cool grey eyes were studying her thoughtfully and Paula gulped down her dismay. She was longing to get down to work and start proving herself and now she'd got to wait another twenty-four hours.

'Be sure and get a good sleep tomorrow, Nurse, so that you'll feel fresh and rested for duty. That's all, thank you.'

It was just about impossible to follow the instructions. Paula walked round and round the park in the morning, trying to make herself tired. But as she had already had a night's sleep she didn't need one in the daytime as well.

After a series of uneasy naps she got up with relief and began to get ready for starting her new life. When she had put on the green-checked uniform dress, over-long and old-fashioned in cut but worn with pride by the nurses at West City, she looked at herself in the mirror.

If only she had earned the right to wear a blue dress and a red belt . . . Passionately she longed to put the clock back and relive the precious wasted months. But it was no good. She must face up to the present and do her utmost to give satisfaction at St Andrews.

It took only a short time to reach the Intensive Care Unit which, Paula remembered, was part of a new addition at the back of the original hospital. The night staff nurse, a pale-faced dark girl, was in conversation with a fair young man wearing a short white coat.

'Hullo! I'm Kirsten Stevens.' She smiled

pleasantly and introduced the houseman. 'This is Tony Carlton. We see a lot of him—unfortunately. Your name's Paula, isn't it? We always use Christian names in the Unit, except when Miss Wallace is around. Even Sister likes us to call her Anne.'

'Hi, Paula!' Tony's blue eyes beneath thick fair lashes studied her with interest and he raised one eyebrow as he noted her small waist and slender legs.

He was making her feel as though he was mentally stripping her clothes off but it was done with a friendly sort of impudence which gave no offence. Nevertheless, Paula tilted her chin slightly as she returned his stare. In the past she had often got into trouble for getting too friendly with housemen. She didn't intend to let it happen here.

'Sister's still on duty,' Kristen was saying. 'You'd better come and meet her.'

Anne Knox was in her late twenties, a plump girl with a riot of red curls on which her elaborate lace-trimmed cap sat uneasily.

'I hope to goodness Miss Wallace will soon let you come on day duty,' she told Paula. 'We really do need you on this ward.'

'Do you have many patients?'

'A dozen, which isn't many compared to some wards, but half of them are in a coma and the others require very careful nursing.' She began to lead the way round and Paula followed. 'Most of them are car accident cases—and some motor cycles, of course.'

They paused by a bed where a boy of seventeen lay inert. 'This one, for instance. His parents gave him a bike for his birthday. He rode it along a busy main road and crashed into a bus. He's been unconscious now for five weeks.'

Paula looked down at the shaven-headed figure. He was so still he might have been a shop-window model, yet he had once been eager and active and full of life. With all her heart she hoped he might become so again.

Conscientiously she tried to store up all that Sister was telling her. And if the apparently lifeless bodies made her shudder she gave no sign of it.

With Laura Middleton, the junior nurse, she began the night routine. ICU patients needed constant care if they were to be kept healthy and, whenever time permitted, the unconscious ones must be talked to, about anything and everything, in the hope that one day a word might penetrate the mental fog which enveloped them.

The hours passed quickly and Paula was surprised when the time came for her midnight meal.

The quickest way to the dining room was by an outdoor route, through the shrubbery. The night air was refreshing after the close warm air of the ward and she walked slowly.

Suddenly a memory dating back to her previous experience of St Andrews shot to the forefront of her mind. The hospital had been built on the site of a nunnery and inevitably there were ghost stories. Wasn't there something about the white floating shape of a nun being seen along this very path?

Paula hesitated and then forced herself to continue. She couldn't possibly go back now. Everyone would laugh.

She had nearly reached the end of the dark narrow path when it happened. Turning a corner she saw before her a vague whiteness moving slowly between the bushes. There was a low eerie moaning followed by heavy breathing.

Momentarily frozen to the ground, she somehow regained the power of movement. Whirling round she fled back the way she had come and burst out of the shrubbery—straight into the arms of another white figure.

But this one was reassuringly solid and a masculine voice demanded sharply, 'What on earth's the matter with you? Anyone'd think you'd seen a ghost.'

CHAPTER TWO

'I DID see a ghost!' Paula struggled to get a grip on herself. 'At least I thought I did,' she added hastily.

'Don't be daft—of course you didn't. It must have been a trick of the light.' The voice was definitely scornful now.

'But there wasn't any light in the shrubbery and that's where the ghost is supposed to walk.'

'Surely you don't believe that old story?'

'Of course not,' she hurried to assert, even though her still thudding heart denied the truth of the statement. 'But I certainly saw something white sort of floating along. Anyone would have been startled.'

'Anyone with a vivid imagination, you mean. Who are you, anyway?' He bent his head and peered into her face. 'I don't think I've seen you before.'

'Paula Garland. I'm new here.' She waited a moment and then continued stiffly, 'Perhaps you'll introduce yourself.'

'Justin Stewart,' he told her briefly.

She looked at him thoughtfully in the faint light and saw a very tall young man with a lean face. His eyes were pits of shadow and she could not discern their colour, but his hair was as black as the night.

'Am I supposed to have heard of you?' she asked.

'I've no idea.' His broad shoulders moved in a faint suggestion of a shrug. 'I'm a registrar on the general surgery team here. Part of our job is to look after the ICU, since the blokes really in charge of it operate from London.'

'Then I suppose you work with Tony Carlton?'

'Yes. Anything else you want to know?'

'No, thank you,' Paula said curtly and then immediately asked another question. 'Where did you suddenly appear from? You weren't in the ward when I left.'

'I reached the lobby just as you closed the door behind you, on my way to do a last round before going to bed. I stepped outside for a breath of air and heard you scream—'

'I didn't scream!'

'I assure you that you did.' There was a gleam of white teeth as he smiled. 'It's a good thing I was here or you might have had hysterics.'

'I've never had hysterics in my whole life—'

'No? Well, there's always a first time. Like me to walk along with you through the shrubbery, or are you going to be a coward and take the other route?'

Paula hesitated. He had made her feel a fool and she hadn't much cared for it. If she chose to walk through the hospital he would despise her even more, and yet—

As she dithered he seized her by the arm and

turned her round so that she was facing the way she had come.

'I'll make up your mind for you. Come on—let's go and find that ghost of yours.'

He was holding her so firmly that she was obliged to keep step with him across the grass, but the shrubbery path was not wide enough for two people to walk abreast. Justin released her as they reached it and marched ahead.

They came to the place where Paula had seen the apparition and there was, of course, nothing there except darkness and faintly rustling leaves. Nevertheless, she couldn't resist a nervous glance over her shoulder as they passed and she was furious when she heard a chuckle from her escort.

Had the man got eyes in the back of his head?

'I'm glad you find it so funny,' she told him tartly.

'My dear girl, it's high time *you* started to find it funny. If you can't laugh at yourself, then all I can say is that I'm sorry for you. You're in for a hard time.'

His superior tone was almost more than Paula could bear. He was talking to her as though she were a student nurse straight from school. Perhaps he even thought that was what she was? The third-year belt wouldn't be very noticeable at night.

The instant they emerged from the shrubbery she halted.

'You needn't come any further. I'm grateful to you for rescuing me and making sure I didn't have hysterics, to say nothing of giving me all that good advice. And now you—you can go to hell for all I care!'

Fleeing from him towards the side door of the hospital she experienced a moment of satisfaction. But by the time she reached the almost empty dining room she had an uneasy feeling that, by losing her temper, she had again made a fool of herself.

Lost in thought, she ate a meal she didn't want and then forced herself to return through the shrubbery. She said nothing about her experience to the other two nurses and by morning she was so tired from lack of sleep that she had almost forgotten it.

It was Tony who reminded her.

Paula was nearing the end of her week of night duty when they met by chance as she returned from a morning walk. Tony was standing by the tennis courts where two rather lazy games were in progress and he turned to greet her with a friendly smile.

'They want their heads examining, bashing a ball about in this weather. What wouldn't I give for a long cool beer!'

'What's stopping you having it?' she asked.

'The pubs are closed and I happen to be on duty. Come and have some coffee with me.'

'I was just off to bed.'

'You've got time for a cuppa first. Coffee won't keep you awake, will it?'

She shook her head. 'Nothing would keep me

awake after the night we've just had. Two new admissions and a death.'

'That poor lad who smashed himself up on his birthday? There was never really any hope for him, you know.'

'I think his parents hadn't given up. They were very much upset.' Paula sighed and then added savagely, 'I *hate* the ICU!'

'Do you?' He sounded surprised. 'I would have thought it was very interesting from a nursing point of view. After all, it's quite a challenge.'

'It's okay when you can see some results, but I miss the personal contact with patients. Those two new ones, for instance, look like being unconscious indefinitely.'

'There's more hope for the boy—he's not on a life-support machine—but I'm afraid he's in pretty bad shape.'

Paula said nothing. She was resolutely trying to put out of her mind the mental picture of those two battered bodies lying in adjoining cots, utterly unaware of their surroundings and each other. The air was sweetly scented with roses and newly cut grass, and she told herself firmly it was a glorious morning and the world was full of life, not death.

'Come and have coffee in the Nurses' Home,' she suggested. 'It's nicer than the dining room.'

Tony agreed at once. 'I'm quite at home there. A regular visitor, you might say.'

'That doesn't surprise me!'

A few minutes later, as they sat in the lounge, he asked a sudden question which jerked her wide awake.

'Seen any more ghosts?'

'Ghosts?' Her eyes widened as she looked at him across a small table. 'What do you know about that?'

But before he could speak the query was answered in her own mind. Justin must have told him. No doubt they had laughed together over her gullibility and absurd fear. Indignantly she burst into speech.

'Don't tell me—I can guess. I'm sure you both found the whole thing wildly amusing.'

Tony grinned at her across his cup. 'Well, yes, it was rather funny. You would have laughed if you'd seen yourself. Rushing off like that yelling at the top of your voice—'

'I didn't yell. I only gave one small scream because I was startled—' She broke off and stared at him suspiciously. 'How do you know all those details? Did Justin give you a full description?'

'Things get around, love,' he said airily.

But Paula was not satisfied. She leaned forward, gazing into his face. Although he looked tired—as housemen always did—he was very attractive, with good features and a nice smile. But there was a twinkle in the blue eyes which made her almost certain she had found her ghost.

'It was *you*,' she accused him. 'You laid in wait deliberately to scare me.'

Tony admitted it without a shadow of shame. 'But I didn't lie in wait. It was a spur of the moment thing—inspiration if you like. I was on my way to the Residency and dwelling happily on thoughts of bed when I heard you leave the Unit. Kirsten was talking to you and voices carry easily at night when there's no wind. It was dead easy to fix up. I merely whipped off my white jacket and waved it slowly across the path, making ghostly noises the while.'

'Of all the silly schoolboy tricks!' Paula's voice was full of scorn. 'Haven't you grown up yet?'

Tony shrugged. 'Maybe it was a bit juvenile, but just think what a houseman's life would be like without some light relief.' He put out his hand and laid it over hers where it rested on the table. 'Am I forgiven?'

'I suppose so.' It was impossible to resist his appeal and she smiled, gently withdrawing her hand at the same time. 'But don't do anything like that again. I don't like being frightened nearly out of my life.'

'I didn't think it would scare you that much and I've felt a bit regretful ever since. Justin told me I ought to be ashamed of myself.'

'Did he guess it was you?' she asked in surprise.

'Oh yes. I suppose it wasn't difficult really. He knows my infantile mind.'

'I can't imagine *him* ever descending to those depths of idiocy,' she said thoughtfully.

Tony raised one eyebrow, a habit which Paula was beginning to find attractive. 'That ought to have been meant as a compliment but it didn't sound that way at all.'

'Didn't it?' She laughed and stood up. 'You can amuse yourself figuring out which way I meant it. I'm off to bed.'

She went to her room feeling she had made a friend. It was difficult for a night nurse to get integrated into the life of a hospital, even at such a small place as St Andrews, and she still felt very much a stranger.

Transferring to day duty at the end of the week was almost like starting all over again, since she was with a different set of nurses. The patients, of course, were just the same although in a normal ward there would have been plenty of difference between night and day.

'It's so difficult to talk to people who can't respond,' she complained one morning after spending five minutes describing her home to Jean, the girl who had been brought in with her boy friend a few nights ago.

'I thought you were making a very good job of it,' said a voice behind her.

Paula spun round and found Justin looking down at her.

'I didn't know you were there. I thought it was

Sister—' She went pink with embarrassment.

'Does it matter that I'm not Sister? I found your conversation very interesting and I expect Jean would have done too if she had been able to hear it, poor lass.'

Paula moved a little farther from the bed. 'I thought you could never be sure they heard nothing?'

'It's good nursing to assume that something might get through to them. After all, that's why they have to be talked to.' He broke off and stood staring down at the girl's unconscious face.

It had been miraculously unmarked by the accident and the terrible injuries to the back of her head were hidden by the bandages. She lay as though deeply asleep, her long lashes lying still on cheeks still faintly tanned.

'She had such pretty hair,' Justin went on, half to himself. 'Long and blonde and with a tendency to curl. There was still some of it left when she was brought here but we had to cut it all off.'

'It will grow again,' Paula said gently.

'Oh yes, of course—if it ever gets the chance.' His lips twisted into a crooked smile. 'Don't take any notice of me. I'm in a sentimental mood.'

'Surely that's rather rare?' she couldn't resist saying.

'Very rare indeed,' he agreed blandly and moved on to where Kevin, Jean's boy friend, lay in a similar coma, except that he was able to breathe without assistance.

He had intrigued Paula by giving her a glimpse of a different man from the one she had so far seen, the cool, methodical and correct young doctor. After that she found herself looking out for some indication that his softer side really did exist but she discovered no sign of it at all.

'He's fine to work with,' Sally Morton, the staff nurse said, 'but a bit inhuman somehow.'

'I bet he's got his sights set on being a consultant by the time he's thirty,' remarked a second-year nurse who, with Paula, made up the normal day staff of the Unit. 'And when he *is* one he'll be stiff and starchy and practically insist on the nurses curtseying when he appears.'

'If you can't find anything more sensible than that to say, Judy, you'd better shut up,' Sally told her tartly. 'Have you done the pressure points yet?'

'I was waiting for Paula to be ready to help me.'

'I'm just coming.'

With patients who were incapable of any movement, pressure points were of enormous importance. The nurses prided themselves on keeping their charges in good condition. But as they worked down the lines of beds, each like an outsized child's cot with the sides up, Paula allowed her mind to drift.

Tomorrow was her day off and she was debating whether to go home or stay at St Andrews and do some studying. She hadn't felt like bookwork when she was on nights, and since then there hadn't been much opportunity. Virtuously, she decided to postpone her visit home and do some work instead.

The weather was continuing warm and Paula settled in the garden with a textbook open on her lap. At first she couldn't concentrate. She looked up every time a bird flew past or a dog barked, or someone came up the drive. But gradually she got some control over her mind and she was deep in a study of different diets when a shadow fell across her book. Justin was standing in front of her.

'Nice to be off duty this lovely weather,' he said enviously.

'I may be off duty but I *am* working.' She waved the book at him.

He sat down beside her and stretched out his long legs. 'Are you free all day?'

'Yes.' And, curiously, she added, 'Why do you ask? So you can go on wallowing in envy?'

'Not at all. I'm about to ask you to come to a party with me tonight.'

'You what?' Paula gasped, scarcely able to believe her ears.

'You heard.'

As she stared at him in amazement he gave her his odd crooked smile and went on to elaborate. 'I have a cousin who's a nurse at West City. She and some friends have recently moved into a flat and they're throwing a party. In a weak moment I promised to attend. Unfortunately I'm temporarily without a partner for that sort of occasion so I've been looking round for someone to go with me.'

'And you think I might do?' Her voice rose indignantly. 'Thanks very much! I don't know when I've felt so flattered.'

Justin turned his head and looked at her in genuine surprise. With a small part of her mind Paula noted that his eyes were a very dark grey and his lashes black like his hair.

'I don't see why you have to be like that,' he complained. 'Surely it's best to be frank?'

'From your point of view, no doubt it is. I'm sure you wouldn't want me to get any wrong ideas. But a girl doesn't much care for being told she's only a makeshift.'

'I'm sorry,' he said after a pause. 'I hadn't looked at it quite like that. But you will come, won't you?'

'No, I won't! You can either go by yourself or find somebody who's so dead keen on parties she doesn't care who takes her so long as she gets there.'

'Like who?' he demanded.

'How should I know? I'm still a stranger here.'

Justin brooded, staring down at his feet. 'I suppose I'd better ring up and say I shan't be coming.'

'Please yourself.'

'My cousin will be furious with me.'

'I expect you'll survive.'

'Probably, but I'm very fond of her and I'd like to

go to her party.' He turned and leaned his arm along the back of the seat, looking into her face. 'Please come, Paula. After all this swotting I reckon you could do with a bit of social life.'

Surprisingly, Paula was suddenly tempted. She had been to plenty of parties at West City during the last few years—too many probably. But the last one seemed a very long time ago and, if she went to this one, she might meet people she knew.

Justin had evidently sensed her irresolution and, wisely, he said nothing more, leaving her to think it out for herself. Abruptly making up her mind, she capitulated.

'On second thoughts, I'm glad you were careful to explain why you were asking me. I think I'll come after all. I've got nothing particular to do this evening.'

If she had expected enthusiastic thanks she was disappointed. Justin merely nodded and announced that he would meet her by the gate at seven o'clock. He then went striding off.

Oddly disconcerted, Paula stared after him and then resolutely returned her attention to her book.

She was ready in good time, wearing a softly draped summer dress in a subtle shade of green, a white shawl flung round her shoulders and her shoulder-length hair brushed until it shone. Justin was already at the gate when she arrived and when she saw his car she gave an involuntary exclamation of surprise and pleasure.

It was very old but in excellent condition and it had an open top.

'I hope you won't hate being blown about,' Justin said as she got in. 'It would be a pity to put the hood up on such a lovely evening.'

Paula agreed eagerly. 'I don't mind the wind. I've hardly ever ridden in an open car before and I'm sure I shall enjoy it.'

'It's not altogether an advantage in London,' he told her, roaring down the road, 'but it's great in open country.'

'I'm sure it is,' she said a little wistfully. Almost certainly she would never have the chance to experience it.

Her hair streaming out behind her head, she sat upright beside him as they left Belton Park and came to a stretch of road where the speed limit was higher. What would it be like, she wondered, to drive at seventy, eighty—even more?

All too soon they were back in the thirty-mile limit and they remained in it until they reached the familiar neighbourhood of West City.

Justin turned into a narrow road lined with tall old houses. 'We're nearly there now. It's just round the corner at the end of this road. Very handy for the hospital.'

She didn't know anyone who lived about here, Paula decided, but almost immediately she was proved wrong.

As Justin drew up at the kerb the noise of the

party floated down to them from the wide open windows, voices, laughter, music. They were making their way up the stairs when it occurred to her to put the question she should have asked right at the beginning.

'Is this just a party for no particular reason? Or are they celebrating something? Someone's birthday perhaps?'

Justin looked up at her from a lower stair. 'Didn't I tell you? My cousin's recently become an SRN. She and some other staff nurses moved into this flat and the party's housewarming and general celebration—' He broke off, suddenly noticing Paula's expression. 'What on earth's the matter?'

'N-nothing.' She turned her back and went on up the last few steps. 'What's your cousin's name?'

'Mary Shipton.' His voice was warm with pride. 'She did wonderfully well in the exam and was awarded the gold medal.'

She might have guessed it, Paula thought bitterly. Although one was fair and the other dark, they were extraordinarily alike. Both tall, good-looking and superior, confident in all they undertook, born to be successful.

CHAPTER THREE

THEY crowded round her—Mary and three other girls whom Paula knew well—all of them surprised to see her.

'How are you getting on in your isolation? I've almost forgotten what it's like at St Andrews.' That was Sarah who had spent two months there at the same time as Paula herself, in their first year.

'I quite like it actually.' Paula smiled, determined to keep her end up.

'But don't you miss West City?' Katie asked. 'We all felt terribly sorry for you when we heard you'd been—well, sort of banished.'

'Which ward are you on?' Julie wanted to know. 'The ICU? Gosh, that's grim!'

'But very rewarding when someone makes a complete recovery,' Mary said in her precise way. She glanced towards Justin, who was talking to a couple of housemen. 'You haven't wasted much time in getting to know my cousin but I suppose it's easy in such a small hospital.'

'I know him very slightly, as a matter of fact.' Paula spoke lightly and carelessly, desperately anxious not to give a wrong impression. 'He was in need of a partner for your party and I happened to be available, that's all.'

'I see.' Mary's tone suggested that she was still puzzled. 'I can't think why but it doesn't matter. I'm sure we're all very pleased to see you, Paula.'

'Thanks. It's nice to be back.' Paula smiled and moved on to join a different group.

As the party began to warm up she found herself relaxing and beginning to enjoy herself. It really *was* nice to be once more in the familiar atmosphere of West City, among people she knew well. No one mentioned the exam and her 'banishment' was not referred to again.

She saw little of Justin, perhaps largely because she did her best to avoid him. There was no room for dancing, and although some of the men and girls paired off, most of them remained in circulation.

Towards midnight people began to leave, since many of them were on early duty, and Justin appeared suddenly at Paula's side.

'Do you think you could tear yourself away?' he asked.

'No problem—I'm on early duty too.' She looked round and located Mary standing near the music centre. 'We'd better say goodbye to your cousin.'

Mary kissed Justin enthusiastically, but to Paula she merely said, 'See you some time, I expect.'

'I doubt it. I don't intend to make a habit of popping back to West City.'

'I'm sure that's very wise of you. There's no future in nostalgia, is there?' Mary told her earnestly.

'What on earth did she mean by that?' Justin asked as they descended the stairs.

'Nothing.' Outside on the pavement, Paula looked accusingly at him. 'Why didn't you tell me she was your cousin?'

'You didn't ask me.'

'I can't think why I didn't. It was quite likely to be someone I knew.'

'West City is a big place,' he pointed out, opening the car door for her. 'There must be plenty of nurses you've never even spoken to. And Mary's a year in advance of you. I was surprised you seemed to know her so well.'

'Her room was next to mine at the Nurses' Home,' Paula said briefly.

'Oh, I see.' Justin appeared satisfied with the explanation. He started the engine and the little car shot down the road.

'I expect you know she got the gold medal,' he went on. 'Nobody in the family was surprised she should do so well because she was always dead keen on nursing and she's just the sort of girl to stick at it and not let social occasions interfere with her study.'

'We can't all rise to those heights of dedication.' Paula stared rigidly ahead as they joined the traffic streaming along the main road.

'Do I detect a slightly acid tone?' Justin asked.

'Perhaps. I'm just not in Mary's class where dedication is concerned.'

'Yet at St Andrews you seem to spend quite a lot of time studying.'

'Only because there's nothing else to do.'

He did not reply and Paula leaned back suddenly and wondered why on earth she was trying so hard to present such an inaccurate picture of herself. It was the old Paula she was describing, not the new one who had been born out of disappointment and bitter regret.

Almost as though he had read her mind, Justin broke the silence abruptly.

'Come off it, Paula—you're not like that.'

'What do you mean?' she asked aggressively. 'You don't know anything about me.'

'I've got eyes in my head and I've seen you in the ward. I'm not saying you're like Mary—she's in a class of her own. But you aren't a don't-care type either. I'm sure of it.'

There was a pause before Paula answered. She had been quite absurdly pleased at his summing up of her character but for some odd reason she didn't want him to know. And so she answered him flippantly.

'Thanks very much! I'm glad that stupid business with the ghost hasn't made you write me off completely.'

'I wouldn't have asked you out tonight if it had,' he said quietly.

There didn't seem to be any answer to that and Paula attempted none. She sat in silence as the miles slipped past and soon they were approaching Belton Park. The High Street shops were dark and deserted and the road leading to St Andrews empty of traffic. Even the hospital showed only a faint glow of light, unlike the great brightly-lit mass of West City presiding over the run-down district around it.

Justin drove into the car park and switched off the engine.

'I'll walk across to the Nurses' Home with you as it's so late,' he announced.

'There's no need—'

'There shouldn't be but I'm afraid there is. Just before you came a nurse returning from some late do had her handbag snatched inside the grounds. And that's much more serious than seeing an amateur ghost.'

He slipped his arm in hers as they strolled past the Residency, where most of the St Andrews doctors lived in bed-sittingrooms or small flats, and crossed the drive in the direction of the nurses' quarters.

There was a light still shining above the entrance but all around it was dark. Paula felt her heart begin to beat a little faster as Justin halted just before they reached the porch. He would presumably expect a goodnight kiss and it was a long time since any man's lips had touched hers.

At first his kiss was gentle, almost casual, and he did no more than slip his arm round her shoulders.

But then everything changed. The other arm came round her and she was drawn close, so close she could feel his heartbeats mingling with her own. The pressure of his mouth was hard and painful, and yet somehow so unbelievably sweet that Paula closed her eyes and surrendered herself to the happiness of the moment.

Justin released her abruptly. He was breathing hard and she sensed that he had no more intended the sudden switch to a deeper emotion than she had herself.

'Sorry!' he said harshly. 'Afraid I got a bit carried away. Forget it.'

But that wouldn't be easy. Paula was disconcertingly aware of that as she went quietly down the corridor to her room. She was shaken to the depths of her being and overwhelmed with a host of memories both sad and happy.

She sat for a long time on the edge of her bed, thinking of the past which had gone for ever, and then swinging back to the more recent disturbing sensations aroused by Justin.

It mustn't happen again, of that there could be no possible doubt. She was free of emotional entanglements now, free to concentrate on nursing and earning the right to wear a red belt. She had fought a bitter battle and won through to a measure of resignation. And *nothing* must be allowed to cause any deviation from her chosen path.

She saw little of Justin during the next few days

and the strange effect of having his arms around her began to recede to the back of her mind.

Then, quite unexpectedly, something occurred in the ward which brought her into close contact with him.

There were no regular visiting hours in the ICU. Parents and families came in and out as they pleased and were always made welcome.

On this particular evening the parents of both Jean and Kevin were sitting beside them, their faces pale and strained. Kevin's mother and father were in their fifties, but Jean's parents were young-looking.

Busy with her evening routine, Paula smiled at them as she passed but Mrs Winton put out a hand to detain her.

'Just a minute, Nurse. We've got something we want to discuss—about our Jean. Is there some place we could go where it's private?'

'There's Sister's office but I'm afraid this is her day off. Staff Nurse Morton is in charge—'

Mrs Winton glanced round the ward. 'She looks very busy and it's really a doctor we want to talk to.' She leaned forward to stare intently at the marble-pale face of her daughter, still totally unaware.

'Mr Browning, the neurologist, will be here on Thursday.'

'He's too high up. I'm a bit scared of him, as a matter of fact.' A ghost of a smile brightened her tired eyes. 'Do you think we could see someone young? More our Jean's generation?'

'There's that nice doctor with dark hair,' her husband put in. 'We both liked him.'

'Dr Stewart? I could get hold of him, I expect.'

During the brief conversation Mr and Mrs Blake had sat silently listening, their faces giving away nothing of their feelings. But now suddenly Kevin's father looked up.

'I don't want any part in this, Nurse. I'd like to make that quite clear. My wife feels the same.'

'Yes, I do,' Mrs Blake said emphatically. 'To my mind it's—it's—' She could not finish the sentence.

'I'm sorry,' Mrs Winton said wearily. 'I truly am dreadfully sorry but I can't help the way I feel. Besides, it's different for you. Kevin isn't on a life support machine.'

Paula was becoming more and more puzzled and apprehensive but she gave no sign of it. She said quietly, 'I'll just tell the staff nurse about it and then phone Dr Stewart. It may take a little while to get him here because he's probably busy in another part of the hospital.'

'I wonder what's in their minds.' Sally looked over Paula's shoulder to where the four unhappy people sat once more wrapped in silence. 'Of course you must do as they ask, and I think you'd better stand by, if they don't object, in case you're needed.'

Justin was located in a surgical ward and he arrived within a few minutes, going straight to the office. When Paula told him what Sally had said he agreed at once that it might be advisable for her to remain at hand.

'But don't make it too obvious. How about making some coffee and then bringing it in after they've had time to explain what's worrying them?'

She gave them ten minutes and then did as he had suggested. She found a tenseness in the small room which could be felt as soon as she opened the door. Mrs Winton was sitting rigidly upright but her husband was slumped in his chair and looked as though he might collapse at any moment.

'Thank you, Nurse.' Justin was at his most formal. 'Will you pour out for us, please?'

Suddenly Mrs Winton said urgently, 'Let's ask her what she thinks. She's not much older than Jean.' She turned to Justin and appealed to him. 'You tell her, Doctor.'

He put a spoonful of sugar in his coffee and stirred it carefully. He said, without looking up, 'Mr and Mrs Winton don't wish their daughter to remain any longer on the life-support machine. They would like it switched off. They also—' he cleared his throat '—wish various organs to be used for transplants.'

Appalled, Paula was temporarily bereft of words. For one desperate moment she longed to rush out of the office and out of the hospital, and to keep on running until she had put as much distance as possible between herself and the Unit.

'Don't you think we're right, Nurse?' Mrs Winton urged. 'There's no sense in torturing ourselves with the thought that Jean may wake up. She'd have done it by now, if she'd been all right. And even if she does come round, she'll only be a cabbage. We don't want that sort of—of living death for her. Do we, Bob?'

Mr Winton shook his head but seemed incapable of words. Paula pulled herself together and struggled to make an adequate reply.

'Quite a lot of people feel like you, Mrs Winton, in similar circumstances, but I do honestly think it's a question only the close relatives can answer. Nobody has any right to try and influence them.'

'Exactly what I said,' Justin reminded them.

'You're not much use, either of you,' Mrs Winton told them bitterly. 'I thought, being young, you'd see it from Jean's point of view. I'm sure she wouldn't want to remain in hospital for the rest of her life, technically alive yet with everything that matters totally dead.' She leaned forward and stared at Paula with eyes bright with unshed tears. 'Think of yourself, Nurse. Is that what *you*'d choose? Life at any price?'

Paula put down the sugar basin with a crash, spilling a little on the desk. For one brief agonising moment she was back in another Intensive Care Unit and someone else was asking her the same question.

She answered as she had done then.

'No, I wouldn't. Not for myself nor anyone I loved. It's far better for undamaged vital organs to be used to give life to someone who might otherwise have died.'

She had spoken quietly but her voice had trembled with emotion to such a degree that Justin looked at her in surprise. Absorbed in their own misery, neither of the Wintons seemed to notice anything unusual.

'Thank you, Nurse.' Mrs Winton blinked rapidly and her voice trembled. 'That's exactly what we hoped to hear.'

'I don't know about *hoped*,' her husband muttered. He stared down at his untasted coffee. 'But I think she's right, all the same.'

'Of course she is, Bob.' She gulped down her unshed tears and sighed heavily. 'I just wish Kevin's parents could see it the way we do.'

'It's different for them, dear. They're not faced with quite the same problem, Kevin being a little less badly injured.'

'I just hope they appreciate how lucky they are, that's all.'

'I don't think lucky is quite the right word. Less unfortunate would sound better.' Ashen-faced he rose to his feet. 'We'd better not take up any more of Dr Stewart's time and I expect the nurse is pretty busy too.'

Leaning forward to put his cup on the desk, he

swayed alarmingly. As Paula took a quick step towards him he slid from her grasp, sending his chair over backwards, and fell in a crumpled heap on the floor.

'Oh dear, oh dear—' His wife went down on her knees beside him. 'It's all been too much for him, poor darling. He was so terribly fond of Jean.'

The little office suddenly seemed terribly crowded and Justin asked Mrs Winton to move back. Together he and Paula loosened her husband's collar and tie and then she opened the window to freshen the air. After a moment their patient stirred and his eyelids flickered.

'Fetch him a dose of sal volatile,' Justin said. 'He'll be all right in a minute.'

She was glad to leave the emotion-charged atmosphere and have something definite to do. As she measured out the dose she found that her hands were shaking and she knew it would be some time before she got over the effects of the last few minutes.

Fortunately she was off duty soon after Jean's parents had left and she walked slowly across the grounds, aware that she ought to go to the dining room for supper but quite unable to face even the thought of food.

As she turned her back on the hospital and stared out across the garden, a door behind her opened and Justin came out.

'That was not an experience I want to repeat in a hurry,' he said with a sigh.

'Nor me—but I shouldn't have let it affect me so much.'

'We're not machines. We can't help sharing other people's emotions at times. I feel pretty shaken myself.'

They were silent for a moment, lost in their own thoughts.

Then Paula said painfully, 'It wasn't only that I shared the Wintons' grief.' She hesitated, feeling a desperate need to talk but very much afraid she might break down if she did so.

'What was it then?' Justin asked, looking down at her intently.

'It—it reminded me of another occasion, rather similar.'

'Have you worked in an Intensive Care Unit before?'

'Yes—at West City, some time ago. But this was at a different hospital and I wasn't working. Someone I knew was unconscious like Jean—after an accident—and his parents decided to have the life-support machine switched off.'

Justin's arm was round her shoulders and she felt the comforting pressure of his hand through the cotton material of her sleeve.

He asked carefully, 'Were you—that is, did the patient mean a lot to you?'

'Yes, but I agreed with the parents. They were so

wonderfully kind and consulted me about it. Not many people would have done that, under the circumstances.'

He did not enquire what those circumstances had been. Instead he held her close for a moment and gently stroked her hair with his free hand.

'I expect this evening brought it all back to you,' he said after a while.

'Yes—horribly!' She sighed and leaned her head against him. 'It all happened months ago—last Christmas—and I was getting over it a bit. That sounds callous but it's not really. I mean, life has to go on.'

'Of course it does.'

With a sudden rush of words she told him about the effect of the tragedy on her career.

'I failed my SRN exam. I suppose I ought to have admitted it when you took me to Mary's party but I was so ashamed of having done so badly. That's why I'm at St Andrews. I have to work here for a year before taking it again.'

'A whole year? That's a bit harsh, isn't it? I would have thought you'd be able to sit it next time.'

'Miss Grieves won't let me.' Paula thought of those bad ward reports but couldn't bring herself to mention them.

'I think you've had a raw deal,' Justin announced firmly.

His words were balm to her wounded spirit, and

his arm about her made her feel warm and pro-
tected. She would have liked to stay like that for a
long, long time.

Justin was the first to stir. He dropped a light kiss
on the top of her head and asked, 'Feeling better
now?'

'Yes, thanks.' Reluctantly she disengaged herself. 'I'd better go in and force some food down.'

'You'll feel better still afterwards,' Justin told
her unromantically.

He had an annoying way of being right, Paula
decided later on. Physically she was restored completely, and even her mental state was much better.

But at the back of her mind there remained a
small nagging thought. She hadn't been entirely
frank with him about that accident six months ago.
Perhaps if she'd told him the whole truth he might
not have been so kind.

CHAPTER FOUR

WHEN Paula reported for duty the following day Jean's bed had been wheeled away. Kevin still lay unconscious, unaware of the tragedy which had taken place.

During the morning, when the pressure of work had eased a little, Justin joined her for a moment in the kitchen.

'I thought you'd like to know that Jean's kidneys are both to be used and also her cornea. Her parents' very brave decision will mean new life to other people. Does that make you feel better about it?'

'Oh yes, it certainly does. Thank you for telling me.' She looked up at him but he was staring across the top of her head.

It was hard at that moment, in spite of his quiet and sympathetic tone, to believe he was the same man who had held her in his arms and comforted her distress. And yet—what else could she have expected, here in the ward kitchen?

Paula gave herself a mental shake and returned to the ward. She was accosted immediately by Pat Milton, a second-year student nurse, who was looking most unusually excited.

'Guess what, Paula! Carol's come round.'

She was referring to a schoolgirl who had been knocked off her bicycle by a juggernaut nearly three weeks ago. No one had expected her to remain unconscious for so long and her condition had been causing some concern.

'I was talking to her,' Pat went on. 'You know Sister's always telling us how important that is but somehow you never *really* think you'll get any response. And then Carol suddenly opened her eyes and looked at me and she asked where she was and what had happened. I've never been so thrilled in my life.'

'Go and tell Sister about it quickly. She'll be tremendously bucked.'

Paula walked swiftly towards the bed where Carol lay to see the miracle for herself. The wide open eyes were clear and full of intelligence, although the girl's memory was still clouded, which was only natural.

A moment later Anne Knox joined them and together they rejoiced though they were careful not to let the patient suspect how worried they had been about her.

'It makes it all worth while, doesn't it?' Anne said as she went off to telephone Carol's parents. 'I know you all find it difficult to talk to someone who doesn't give any sign of being able to hear but it does pay dividends sometimes.'

There was an atmosphere of hope in the ward throughout that day. As she helped to turn inert bodies and attended to their never-ending physical needs, Paula found it increasingly easy to put out of her mind the agonising scene which had taken place on the previous evening.

You had to balance one thing with another where nursing was concerned, she told herself firmly, and it was absolutely true that tragedy played a very small part in the general scene.

As the summer days slipped by she stuck closely to her appointed path. Work and study without much relaxation was a dull programme and yet she was conscious of an increasing feeling of happiness. She didn't try to analyse it; she merely assumed that it was due to having got her life under control and come to terms with it.

It was Tony who showed her that she wasn't quite so fully in charge as she had imagined.

It happened one night. Paula had been reading in bed and had dropped off to sleep with the book open and the bedside light still on. A soft tap on the door roused her instantly.

For a moment she was startled and made no move. Then, thinking someone might be feeling ill and need her help, she slipped out of bed just as the tap came again, a little louder. In her filmy nightdress, her hair tumbled about her face, she opened the door and peeped out.

She had taken it for granted that the visitor would be a nurse but, to her utter astonishment, Tony Carlton stood there.

'Tony! What on earth are you doing here in the Nurses' Home?'

'Hi, Paula!' He grinned at her wickedly and then grimaced as there was a movement behind him.

A young nurse looking worried and dishevelled, with her long hair half hiding her face, came forward and Paula saw that it was Pat Milton. She immediately burst into agitated speech.

'I'm terribly sorry, Paula. We could see your light under the door and we're in the most awful fix. You've got to help us!'

'I might if I knew what you wanted. You'd better come in.' Leaving the door open she crossed to a chair and picked up her dressing-gown. 'What's the matter?'

'I should have thought that was obvious,' Tony said cheerfully. 'I want to get out of here.'

'What's stopping you then?' she asked, deliberately obtuse.

'Don't ask daft questions, Paula. You know perfectly well I can't go out by the front door because the Warden always keeps the key when she locks up at night—the mean old so-and-so. There's another in a glass box in case of fire but I could hardly smash that and help myself.'

'I thought all male visitors were supposed to be out by eleven.'

He raised one eyebrow and looked down his nose at her. 'So what? This wouldn't be the first time I've climbed out of a window but Pat's room is on the second floor and I'm no cat burglar. *Now* do you see what all this is in aid of?'

'You want to get out through *my* window.'

He turned to his girl friend. 'The penny's dropped at last.'

'Please,' she begged. 'It doesn't matter at all to you but it's enormously important to us. The Warden sleeps with her ears out on stalks and I'd get into a hell of a row if it was discovered I'd had a man in my room.'

'My window squeaks,' Paula said flatly. 'She'll probably hear anyway.'

'For goodness' sake, stop messing about,' Tony said irritably. 'The old girl sleeps on the other side of the house and it's perfectly safe to use this escape route. I ought to know. The nurse who had this room before you was a friend of mine.' He moved purposefully across the room and drew the curtains back.

'I don't seem to have much option,' Paula said unhappily. 'I can't stop you using my window but I hope you won't do it again. It's too risky.'

'Who for?'

'Both of us.'

'You could always pretend you were sound asleep and knew nothing about it.'

'I wouldn't stand much chance with an obviously phoney story like that.'

Pat had been listening anxiously and she now

interrupted. 'Wouldn't it be a good idea to put the light out?'

Paula leapt across the room and switched off the bedside lamp. What a fool she'd been not to think of that! She watched nervously as Tony climbed out onto the sill, waved his hand nonchalantly and dropped to the ground.

'I'm terribly grateful to you,' Pat was saying. 'We really were in a spot.'

'It shouldn't have happened,' Paula said curtly, re-drawing the curtains and again putting on the light. 'In future don't let yourselves get so carried away you forget all about the time.'

Listening to herself, she was ashamed. She knew only too well how easily that sort of situation could occur and if her own career hadn't been in danger because of her assistance, she would have been much more sympathetic.

It was so desperately important that no shadow of incorrect behaviour should touch her just now.

The younger nurse went pink and lowered her lashes. 'It wasn't what you think,' she insisted. 'We were—were just talking.'

Paula smiled and raised her eyebrows slightly. 'You'll have to think of a better one than that if Tony is seen.'

'You don't really think there's any risk of that?'

'It could happen.'

Pat flung her an anguished glance and scurried away. Back in bed, Paula tried to woo sleep and found it elusive. The incident which had just taken place was the sort of thing she must avoid at all costs. With all her heart she hoped no one had been abroad late enough to see Tony climbing out of her window.

For a few days she was wary but no reference was made by anyone to what had occurred and gradually her sense of security returned. Once more she experienced the content which she had been aware of before her midnight adventure.

Even so, there were odd occasions when she felt a strange inner restlessness. One of these occurred on a particularly beautiful evening when she had come off duty at five-thirty.

The sun still shone brilliantly and a gentle breeze rustled the leaves of the trees. Wandering among the flower beds, Paula longed for something interesting to do. It was an evening for going out to some attractive place with some special person. It was definitely not an evening for watching TV or poring over textbooks.

Her thoughts were far away and she was startled when she found Justin confronting her.

'Off duty early?' he asked casually.

'Yes. It was one of my days for working all the morning and through the afternoon.' As he made no further comment she continued conversationally. 'It's a gorgeous evening, isn't it? I'm glad I haven't got to work.'

'I'm free too.' He hesitated and then went on

with a rush, 'I was just thinking it would be great to
drive out into the country—perhaps even as far as
the coast. It wouldn't take all that long.'

'Really?' Paula exclaimed, since something
seemed to be expected of her.

'Not in my car.' He grinned and suddenly looked
almost as young as Tony. 'I suppose Southend is the
nearest place but there are others, smaller and
quieter.'

It was obviously her cue to say lightly, 'Sounds
super—I hope you enjoy yourself,' and walk on.
But instead she seemed rooted to the spot and
tongue-tied as well.

Justin looked at her thoughtfully and seemed to
make up his mind. 'If you're not doing anything
special, Paula, why don't you come as well? I mean,
it's hellish dull going off for a drive by oneself. I'd
be glad of your company.'

Her heart leapt and the beautiful evening suddenly seemed even lovelier. At that moment she
could think of nothing more desirable than an
outing to somewhere where water flowed—cool,
clear and refreshing.

She said quickly, 'Oh, Justin, I'd adore it! It's
been so hot in the ward all day and I kept thinking
I'd like to go to some place right away from Belton
Park, just for a little while.'

'Go and get changed then, and join me in the car
park. Better bring something warm—it's always
colder near the coast.'

She was ready in five minutes, wearing jeans and a yellow tee shirt and carrying a sweater. Justin was already in his car and she joined him with a delicious feeling of happy anticipation.

They spoke little as they drove out of London, and when Justin was able to speed up, the noise of the wind rushing past their ears made conversation almost impossible. Paula sat back and enjoyed it, not caring now where they went—whether to the sea or elsewhere. Content just to be there.

After skirting a large town they turned towards the east coast. Soon they were crossing marshes which stretched emptily for miles, and then a slight rise brought them to an overgrown village near the mouth of a wide river.

Paula roused herself. 'What's this place called?'

'Seagate,' Justin told her. 'We used to come here when I was a kid. My father was mad on sailing and we had a chalet for a whole month every summer. We were allowed to mess about in boats to our hearts' content.'

'Sounds lovely.'

'Yes, it was great.' He drove slowly down a wide main street and turned along the road behind a row of huts at the edge of a sandy beach. 'Are you hungry? There used to be a fairly good hotel at the end of this.'

'I wasn't when we left Belton Park but all that fresh air has made me starving,' Paula admitted.

'Let's eat then.'

She looked doubtfully at the smart modern building they were approaching. 'Doesn't it seem a bit daft to drive all this way to see the sea and then go indoors as soon as we get here? I'm sure I could exist on a bar of chocolate until we get back.'

'Maybe you could but not me.' He swung the wheel and the little car swept into the car park. 'You've got a point though. Tell you what, let's go in the bar and see if we can get something in a basket. Then we can take it away and eat out-of-doors. How about that?'

Paula at once accepted the compromise and they entered the half-empty bar of the hotel and joined the few people at the counter.

While Justin ordered drinks and food she looked round. The owners had made an attempt to reproduce the atmosphere of a village inn. There were old-fashioned weapons—made of plastic—on the walls and imitation oak beams. An imitation log fire glowed on the hearth, fortunately giving out no heat, and above their heads a collection of beer mugs hung from the ceiling.

A little later, carrying a basket each, they went out again and began to walk along the road which led to the marina up river.

'Have you got any objection to staring at boats while we eat?' Justin asked. 'It's much more interesting than looking at a grey empty sea.'

'I'm sure it is but don't expect me to make intelligent comments,' Paula warned.

'I wouldn't be much good at that myself. I haven't sailed since we used to come here all those years ago.'

'Did you know then that you would take up medicine?' she asked as they settled down on the grassy bank.

Justin shook his head. 'I was supposed to be going into the family business. My father is a builder and does very well out of it. There was a good deal of opposition when I suddenly announced that I wanted to go off in an entirely different direction. Luckily I've got a younger brother who was prepared to carry on with tradition.'

Paula wrapped a paper napkin carefully round her portion of chicken and began to eat it hungrily. Behind them, in the dinghy park, the breeze set all the halyards rattling, but the noise, far from being obtrusive, merely seemed part of the peaceful scene. In front of them the smooth water was dotted with larger boats anchored for the night. Voices called to each other and oars creaked in rowlocks, and on the pebbly shore seagulls squabbled briefly over some scraps.

'I've never been anywhere like this before,' she said contentedly when they had finished their meal. 'It's all strange and interesting and—and romantic.'

'I don't know about romantic.' Justin laughed. 'You're seeing it under near perfect conditions, don't forget. It's not so good when a cold nor'easter is blowing or it's pouring with rain or ghostly with fog.'

'It's romantic this evening anyway,' Paula insisted, and caught her breath as he put his hand over hers where it lay idly on her lap.

'Is it the place—or is it us?' he asked softly.

Her heart was thudding but she managed to answer him casually. 'I suppose even somewhere awful like—well, like Liverpool Street Station, for instance, would be romantic to some people if they were interested in trains. I'm very influenced by places, aren't you?'

Justin's grip tightened. 'So do you think the fact that I want to kiss you very badly is entirely due to our surroundings?'

'Could be,' she managed to falter.

But it wasn't the place which was making *her* feel the way she did. It was Justin himself, his long lean body and dark good looks. His face was so close that she could see the pale gold tips to his black lashes and, on one temple just below his hair, a tiny scar.

Staring at it intently because she daren't look into the clear grey depths of his eyes, Paula touched it gently with one finger. 'How did you get this?'

'Fell off my bike when I was eight. I had to have five stitches and boasted about it for weeks afterwards.' He pushed her back gently into the long grass and turned so that he could look down at her. 'Paula—Paula darling, don't try and keep me at a distance with words. You as good as admitted you were feeling romantic.'

'I was talking about the place—you know I was,' she protested, struggling to sit up.

'Stop playing games, love.'

He was half smiling and he kissed her lightly. Convinced that she could handle it, Paula yielded to her own longing and lay still.

And suddenly she felt the full weight of his body on hers. Her defences collapsed and she eagerly surrendered her lips to his urgent demand. As passion leapt within her she shut her eyes and locked her arms behind his neck, forcing him into closer and closer contact.

They lay like that for a long time, hidden in the grass, alone and secret on their patch of river bank even though the clubhouse was only a hundred yards away.

Eventually Justin rolled away and lay on his back, staring up into the darkening sky.

'You're quite a girl, Paula, under that cool exterior. Do you realise how much I wanted to make love to you properly?'

'I wouldn't have let you,' she said quickly.

'No? I've got an idea you wanted it too.'

She was silent as, in her own mind, she admitted the truth of what he had said. She *had* wanted it—desperately—and if Justin's control had not been so good she might have given way, in spite of her firm assertion to the contrary.

'It would have spoilt the evening,' she said eventually.

'Perhaps. And, on the other hand, it might have enhanced it—for the time being.' His voice was very serious. 'But I think we would both have regretted it.'

'Yes.' Although she agreed with him she didn't care to hear him state his opinion so emphatically. 'Oughtn't we to start the run back to London?'

Justin jumped to his feet and held out his hand to pull her up. 'Okay, let's be on our way. Anything after this could only be an anti-climax.'

But the sense of anti-climax already lay heavy on Paula's spirit. As she followed him silently to the road she was obliged to acknowledge that he really did regret the violent emotions of the last hour, even though he had kept a grip on himself.

It was humiliating, to say the least, to have to admit secretly that her own feelings were so totally different. For her the violence of her own turbulent response had been a shock. But certainly not something she regretted.

CHAPTER FIVE

THE first time Justin visited the ICU patients after the trip to Seagate he appeared totally unaware of Paula's existence, even though the ward was an extremely informal one with plenty of conversation between doctors and nurses.

She had tried to school herself to expect no more than that, and yet was quite extraordinarily disappointed to find she was being ignored. Anxious not to let him think she was hovering in the hope of receiving some attention, she found jobs to do in that part of the Unit which was farthest from where he stood talking to Anne Knox by Kevin's cot.

The boy still lay unconscious, breathing regularly and deeply. He had been in a coma for a long time now and the nurses at least had begun to feel that there was less hope of his recovery.

'I don't know how his parents stick it,' Tony said one day to Paula when they happened to meet as she was going for her coffee break. 'Sitting day after day beside his bed would drive me crackers.'

'I suppose—in a way—they've got used to it. And they've never let themselves stop thinking that Kevin will one day open his eyes and recognise them.'

He was silent for a moment, unusual with him, and then changed the subject. 'By the way, I never thanked you for getting me out of a very awkward spot a few nights ago. I was really very grateful.'

'So you ought to be,' Paula said severely. 'If Miss Wallace ever got to hear of it there'd be a most awful row and we'd all be involved.'

'She obviously hasn't so why worry?'

'Just so long as it doesn't happen again.' She paused and then asked curiously, 'Are you and Pat going steady, or was that occasion a sort of one-off affair?'

'My dear girl, I always take care not to go steady with anyone. Take 'em as they come, that's my motto, and I'm sure a sensible person like you will agree it's the right one for a houseman in his first job.'

'Oh yes—provided nobody gets hurt by it.'

'I don't think anyone would take me seriously,' Tony said complacently.

'You should know.'

'But if you're really concerned about Pat, how about coming out with me yourself, just to show her the sort of bloke I am?'

The effrontery of it made Paula burst out laughing. 'Was that a genuine offer?' she enquired lightly.

'Of course it was. My offers are always genuine— at the time.' He grinned down at her cheerfully.

Paula's amusement faded as she thought about

it. Justin had continued to treat her as if she didn't exist and she was both annoyed and hurt by it. No doubt it was silly of her to feel that way but she couldn't help it.

'Maybe I'll take you up on that, Tony. What sort of offer had you in mind?'

She was not surprised when it immediately became clear that he had been talking carelessly and casually for he looked slightly taken aback. But, being Tony, he quickly rallied.

'There's a good film on at the Ritz, so I've heard. Let's go and see it together the next time I have a few hours off.'

'Okay,' Paula agreed. 'If I can manage to be free at the same time.'

By means of changing her duty time with another third year nurse, she contrived it. She was feeling less and less enthusiastic about the arrangement, but obstinacy and a dislike of letting anyone down prevented her from backing out.

'Sorry I haven't got a car,' Tony said as they set forth. 'Can you manage to walk as far as the High Street?'

'Of course I can. I often do it.'

'Perhaps someone will give us a lift,' he went on hopefully. 'We haven't got all that much time.'

It was normal practice for those with cars to offer lifts to people without, since the hospital was not on a bus route. As they walked quickly along the dead straight road and not even the faintest breeze stirred the plane trees, Paula, too, wished someone would come along and pick them up.

Suddenly her ears caught the sound of a car coming up behind them. A sports car, without a doubt.

Tony glanced over his shoulder. 'Here's a bit of luck! I thought it sounded like Justin and I was right. Cheer up, Paula—you'll soon be able to take the weight off your feet.'

The car was slowing down. It drew up beside them and Tony opened the door.

'Thanks a lot,' he said enthusiastically. 'We shall just about make it in time for the big picture now.'

Paula forced herself to look round, to add her thanks to her escort's and get in beside Justin. He had looked at her silently and very briefly but their eyes had met. She hoped she had managed to keep her own blank, but she was shaken to the depths by what she glimpsed in his.

Pain, bewilderment, reproach? It just wasn't possible that all these emotions had been mingled and visible during that one short moment.

There was no reason in the world why he should feel like that. He'd made it very plain that the outing to Seagate was to have no sequel and she was entitled to go out with anyone she chose.

She could feel his shoulder pressed hard against her own in the small space available. With every nerve she was conscious of his nearness. On her other side Tony, equally close, seemed scarcely to exist in spite of the fact that he chattered non-stop during the short drive. He wanted to know all about the car, asking what its maximum speed was and how many miles it did to the gallon.

Justin answered him curtly, using as few words as possible, but he seemed unaware of any restraint, or of the undercurrents which were so unhappily obvious to Paula.

They got out at the corner of the High Street and walked the few yards to the cinema.

'Funny mood he was in tonight,' Tony said, showing more perception than Paula had given him credit for. 'I wonder what was wrong.'

She did not know herself and certainly wouldn't have told him if she had. In spite of the fact that they had arrived at the cinema in good time, she was bitterly regretful of the whole incident. She had accepted Tony's invitation with some idea of proving—to herself—that she didn't care in the least about Justin's attitude towards her. It was already only too plain that she wasn't going to prove anything of the sort.

They had seats in the back row and Tony immediately put his arm round her. She didn't mind that but before long she was kept very busy fending off his wandering hands.

'Relax, can't you?' he muttered in her ear. 'I brought you out for an enjoyable evening.'

'It would be enjoyable if you'd let up a bit,' Paula whispered back. 'It's a very good film—what I've been able to see of it. You should try watching it yourself.'

He did not give up easily but eventually—in spite of a muttered comment she didn't catch—appeared to resign himself to accepting her advice. Although he kept his arm round her, he really did give his attention to the screen.

'I'm sorry if taking me to the cinema has turned out to be a dead loss from your point of view,' she said lightly as they strolled back to the hospital.

'It wasn't quite what I'd expected,' Tony admitted, 'but perhaps I was an optimist to hope for anything different. You're a rum girl, Paula. Did you know that?'

'In what way rum?' she demanded.

'Well, kinda self-contained. You don't let yourself go.'

But she hadn't been self-contained at Seagate. She had let herself go in a way that she was beginning to feel she must try hard to forget.

'I can't help wondering whether you've got a bloke in your life none of us knows about. Someone you're in love with. That would account for your cool don't-touch-me manner. Have you, Paula?'

She was silent for so long that he added apologetically, 'Okay—forget it. Sorry I asked.'

'It's all right. I was just thinking.' And wondering how much to tell him, but she didn't say that aloud. 'I used to be in love with someone but he was killed in a car crash.'

'Gosh—that's awful! No wonder you're not that keen on having it off with someone else. How long ago did it happen?'

'Quite a while now—during the winter, as a matter of fact.'

'You can't mourn him for ever, you know,' he said awkwardly.

'No, of course not, but it takes time to get over anything like that. It was a terrible experience, particularly as I was involved in the crash too.'

Tony took her hand and squeezed it, and they walked on in silence. He was really very nice beneath the surface, Paula reflected. She wouldn't find it at all difficult to get quite fond of him.

'Thank you for taking me out,' she said formally as they said goodnight outside the Nurses' Home.

He bent his head and kissed her lightly on the lips. 'I'll do it again one day if you're a good girl, and I promise to behave myself impeccably as well.'

'Do you think you could manage it?' She laughed and went indoors.

Afterwards, sitting on her bed and reviewing the conversation, she felt guilty. Although she had said nothing which wasn't true, she had deliberately given a false impression of her relationship with Alan Somerton.

Their affair—which neither of them had regarded as serious—had been almost over when he was killed. But the tragic circumstances of his death had left a scar on her heart which would probably be there for ever.

None of this had anything to do with her objection to Tony's caresses. The reason was a different one, and not something she cared to acknowledge even to herself.

Only occasionally, perhaps as she lay awake on a hot summer night did she admit the truth—that she now knew the real meaning of love. At all other times she kept her secret locked safely away in her heart. No one—least of all Justin—must ever guess what a fool she had been.

She was happiest when working in the Unit, which she had so much disliked at first. It was strange—and almost uncanny—what a strong bond could be forged between a patient who was totally insensible and the girl who nursed him.

Paula felt like that with Kevin. As she washed and fed him she talked to him all the time, no longer daring to hope for a response but keeping it up because to cease would be to admit defeat.

One day she got her reward.

She was in charge of the ward at the time. It was early afternoon and—in a normal ward—it would have been the patients' rest hour. Paula went round the beds, checking each patient's condition, even though she knew it all by heart. Everything was as usual until she came to where Kevin lay. It was then that she got a tremendous shock. His eyes were open.

They stared at each other, equally surprised.

'You look like a nurse.' His voice was weak but clear. 'That means I must be in hospital—'

'I *am* a nurse, love.' She pulled herself together and took his wrist, automatically beginning to count the pulse rate.

'I don't understand,' he said fretfully. 'I don't seem able to remember—Have I been ill?'

'Very ill but you're better now.' She smiled at him and thought with dread of how much he would have to be told when he was stronger. 'Would you like a drink? Milk perhaps, or orange juice?'

His thin ashen-pale face twisted into a faint smile. 'I'd rather have beer.'

'Sorry! We only keep alcoholic drinks for medical purposes. Lie still for a minute and I'll bring you something which will make you feel more able to cope.'

She was quickly back with a glass of milk mixed with a patent food, but before returning she had taken a moment to phone through to the switchboard and ask that a doctor should be sent to the Unit as soon as possible.

It was the first time since he was brought to St Andrews that he had received nourishment by the normal method instead of either intravenously or through a tube. Paula slipped her arm beneath his head and raised him carefully but he drank only a very little.

'My mouth feels as though I'd been on an all-night binge. I don't want any more now.'

She did not press it. When she had lowered him gently he asked another question.

'Why haven't I got a pillow? And what are all those bars for? Looks like you've got me in a kid's cot.'

'You were unconscious for some time. Under those circumstances we always put the sides up. It wouldn't be safe otherwise.'

Kevin accepted that and lay quiet for a moment, obviously thinking deeply and struggling to make sense of what he had been told.

'You said I'd been unconscious for some time,' he recalled. 'What did you mean? A whole day perhaps?'

'Longer than that.' Paula glanced round rather desperately, hoping to see either Justin or Tony approaching.

It was not her job to deal with this kind of situation, but since Sister was off duty and the staff nurse had gone off to a late lunch, she had no alternative. She couldn't refuse to answer questions for that would certainly have a bad effect on the patient.

'How long?' he demanded, his voice suddenly much stronger.

'I'm not sure exactly. More than a month.'

'Good God!' His blue eyes, set in long dark lashes, were wide and stricken. 'But whatever was the matter with me? Illnesses don't usually cause such long periods of unconsciousness. And why can't I remember anything about it?'

A movement at the other end of the ward caught her eye and she turned round thankfully. Justin was coming towards her with the long stride which gave no appearance of haste and yet got him quickly to wherever he wanted to be.

'So you're awake at last!' He smiled down at Kevin, betraying nothing of the amazement he must have felt. 'And I expect you want to know what's been happening to you.'

As Paula had done, he put his fingers on Kevin's wrist and kept them there as he continued speaking.

'You were in a car accident and got rather battered about the head, which is why you've temporarily lost your memory. It will almost certainly gradually come back, at least to a certain extent, but it doesn't matter if you don't remember everything. I'm sure you don't really want to be reminded of anything so unpleasant as a car crash.'

'I can't remember anything at all about an accident,' Kevin said with a desperate note in his voice. 'Were my parents involved?'

Paula caught her breath. They were on very dangerous ground indeed now. Across the bed Justin's eyes met hers briefly. There was a query in them and she understood that he wanted to know whether Jean had been mentioned. Imperceptibly—as far as Kevin was concerned—she signalled an answer.

'Oh no, your parents are perfectly all right,' Justin told him. 'They've been visiting you regularly all this time, sitting here and talking to you and never getting even the faintest response. They'll be over the moon when they hear you've come round at last.'

'Poor Mum and Dad. I bet they've been through hell,' Kevin murmured weakly.

'They'll soon forget about that when they hear the good news. Nurse will go and phone your home now, so they know what to expect when they come to see you. We don't want to give them too big a shock.'

It was one of the most enjoyable tasks Paula had ever undertaken, even though Kevin's mother—after a moment of incredulity—burst into tears and was unable to continue the conversation.

Replacing the receiver, she turned round to find Justin behind her.'

'It makes it all worth while, doesn't it?' he said, half to himself. 'All the endless night and day care for weeks, the terrific effort to keep up hope in the relatives—'

'All those awful one-sided conversations!' Paula smiled, happy because of what had happened and because she was talking to Justin.

'How much longer have you got in the Unit?' he asked.

'Until the end of August. I don't know where I shall be sent then.'

'But you'll still be at St Andrews?'

'Oh yes. I'm here for a year. I thought I'd already told you that but perhaps you'd forgotten.'

'Yes, you did tell me. I just wanted to make sure I'd really remembered it.'

As Paula stared at him he gave her a smile of great sweetness and warmth, and then turned away. Left alone in the office, she snatched a moment to regain her composure.

What a strange unpredictable man he was . . . Most of the time he seemed scarcely aware of her existence, but just now it had really seemed as though her remaining at St Andrews was of importance to him.

It was an illusion, of course, like everything else. But it was nice while it lasted.

The memory of it remained with her for the rest of the day. As she shared in the general rejoicing at Kevin's return to life, she was conscious of a small inner happiness. Helping to move his bed into a side ward, away from his depressing companions, she found herself singing under her breath.

'You sound very cheerful,' he commented. 'Is it because of me?'

'Of course!' She smiled and patted his hand where it lay, white and useless-looking, on the bedspread.

In his new surroundings, with plenty of flowers

and gifts sent by friends, he began to make rapid progress. Soon he could remember details of his home, and his parents were overjoyed by the return to normality.

But he still did not mention his girl friend and everyone had been warned not to refer to her.

'I think he will remember her eventually,' Anne Knox said. She brushed back a lock of her curly red hair and looked worried. 'I'm afraid I can't tell you how to cope if I shouldn't happen to be here. You'll have to do the best you can.'

It happened quite suddenly one morning about ten o'clock. The man who brought newspapers to the patients had just supplied one to Kevin, who had expressed a wish to catch up with the news.

He sat up in bed, his head bent studiously over the spread out sheets. His hair—dark brown and slightly wavy—had grown again and he looked very different from the shaven-headed patient whom Paula had first known.

She paused by his bed to re-arrange the flowers on his locker and glanced down at the newspaper.

'Anything interesting?'

There was no answer for a moment and then he looked up at her, his face pale and drawn.

'Nurse—I saw a name in the paper and it was so familiar. But I—I can't think why.'

Paula's heart missed a beat. This was it. Every instinct she possessed was warning her of trouble.

'What name was it?' she asked quietly.

'Jean.' Kevin repeated it under his breath. 'Jean. Why does that particular name have such a strange effect on me?'

'Perhaps you knew someone called that?'

'I reckon I must have. Oh God—I wish I could remember who it was. I'm sure it's important to me.'

'It will come back to you before long, I expect. Don't try too hard now or you'll give yourself a headache.'

He ignored her advice. Frowning, he stared into space, saying the name over and over to himself, and Paula knew this was her cue for going straight to Sister and reporting the state of affairs in the side ward.

Reluctant to leave him, she moved hesitantly towards the door, and at that moment Kevin gave a cry of anguish which went straight to her heart.

'Jean! It's all come back into my mind—the accident—everything!' He stretched out his arms in urgent appeal. *'What happened to Jean?* Why does nobody ever talk about her? I've got to know!'

CHAPTER SIX

PAULA crossed the room swiftly. Sitting down on the edge of the bed—there were no bars now—she put her arms round Kevin and held him close.

'Hush now, love. Just rest quietly and I'll tell you all about it.'

'She's dead, isn't she?' He turned his face towards her and pressed it against her breast. 'She must be because I know she's not in the ward, and if she'd been okay she'd have come to see me. We were engaged, you see—going to be married as soon as it could be fixed up.'

Paula thought rapidly and dismissed the life support machine entirely from her mind. Better that he shouldn't know about that, at least for the present.

'Jean was much more badly hurt than you, Kevin. There was never any real hope that she would recover consciousness, and even if she had lived she would have been—been just a cabbage. You wouldn't have wanted that for her, I'm sure.'

'So she *is* dead—and I'm alive. But what good is my life going to be without her? I loved her so much and now I've killed her. I was driving, you know.' He lifted his head and his anguished gaze held Paula's. 'How am I going to be able to live with that?'

She said quietly but very firmly, 'You mustn't blame yourself in any way. We were told details of the accident at the time and I know a car crossed the central reservation and came right into you. You couldn't do a thing about it.'

'But I'd persuaded Jean to go out that evening. She wanted to stay at home and wash her hair—she had such lovely hair—' He broke into uncontrollable sobbing, his face again hidded against Paula's shoulder.

Someone else had said that, she remembered as she held him, murmuring soft words of comfort as if he had been an unhappy child. Justin had mentioned Jean's hair the day after the two young people had been brought into the ICU.

Justin . . . She glanced up and saw him standing there, looking at her, and at his side Miss Wallace, the Nursing Officer in charge at St Andrews. And on her face there was an expression of acute disgust and indignation.

'What exactly is going on in here, Nurse?' she asked icily. 'What have you done to upset the patient like this?'

Paula disengaged herself and stood up, and Kevin made a great effort to control himself.

'I did nothing, Miss Wallace.' Her tone was quiet but resentment smouldered beneath the lashes she hastily lowered. 'I was only doing my best to—to cope.'

'I hardly think it was necessary to go to such

lengths. However, I don't propose to discuss it now. Come and see me in my office when you are off duty.'

With cheeks an angry scarlet Paula moved away from the bed. They both stood aside to give her room to pass them. As she came level with Justin he spoke to her in a low voice.

'He's remembered, hasn't he?'

'Yes.'

'It would have been better to have fetched Sister.'

'I daresay but I didn't have time.' Without looking at him, she went into the corridor and closed the door behind her.

There was bitterness and rebellion in her heart when she went to Miss Wallace's office. She had tried so hard to keep out of trouble since coming to St Andrews and she still believed she had done the only possible thing in staying with Kevin to comfort him.

The Nursing Officer was writing something and she kept Paula waiting while she finished it. Then she looked up and studied her thoughtfully.

'Perhaps you would like to give me your version of that extraordinary scene?' she suggested.

Paula did so. She had had time to think what she would say and she spoke quietly and briefly, making no excuses for herself because she felt that none were needed.

When she had finished Miss Wallace frowned. 'I

quite understand it was an emotional occasion, Nurse, but it wasn't your place to deal with it. Sister was on duty and she is older than you and much more experienced. She would have been able to handle the unhappy boy without indulging in unsuitable caresses. When I came into the room I thought for a moment I had interrupted a lovers' embrace.'

Unsuitable caresses . . . She was making the genuine tenderness which Paula had felt out to be something disgusting.

She said quickly, 'I'm sorry, Miss Wallace. My only intention was to—to comfort and I did what seemed best at the time. I didn't feel it would be right to leave Kevin alone while I fetched Sister. After all, the ordinary rules of nursing don't always apply in the Intensive Care Unit.'

'That's true, up to a point, but the sort of behaviour I witnessed today was going much too far and I know your Sister would agree with me.' She paused, tapping the desk sharply with the end of her pen. 'I shall be keeping an extra keen eye on you in future, Nurse Garland, so you had better be very careful indeed. You may go now.'

Paula left the office seething with indignation. She had done nothing to be ashamed of—she was as convinced of that now as she had been at the beginning. In fact, she suspected that she would do exactly the same again if the occasion should arise.

She poured it all out to Sally Morton that evening

as they went off duty together, and was listened to sympathetically.

'It was hellish bad luck that Miss Wallace should be doing a round just at that particular moment, Paula. She's a very good Administrator but I don't think she could ever have been a good nurse in the fullest sense. The rules have to be bent now and then—everybody knows that.'

Paula agreed sombrely, glad to have someone on her side but unhappily aware that she couldn't afford to be the person who bent them.

She was off duty in the morning but she woke early, still feeling thoroughly disturbed. After wandering round the garden and finding it too small to contain her restless spirit, she decided to go for a walk in the park.

It was a pretty place, with bright flowerbeds and a lake where vari-coloured waterfowl swam lazily. Feeling a little soothed by the gentle scene, Paula sat down under a tree and watched some small children throwing breadcrumbs to the birds.

She was still there half-an-hour later when Justin came walking that way. He halted abruptly when he saw her, hesitated a moment and then sat down.

'Mind if I join you?'

'It's a free country,' she said carelessly but softened it with a smile. 'What on earth are you doing here in the middle of the morning?'

'It's my day off and I'm undecided what to do with it.'

'It won't help you to make up your mind, sitting under this tree. It's made me feel thoroughly lazy.'

'And what's wrong with that?'

'I didn't say there was anything wrong with it but it hasn't encouraged me to get into the mood for going on duty after lunch. Specially after what happened yesterday,' she added ruefully.

'Meaning that unfortunate scene with Kevin? I'm afraid Miss Wallace took a dim view of it. Did she make herself very unpleasant afterwards?'

Paula grimaced. 'It could have been worse. I don't know what she'd say if she knew I wasn't in the least repentant.' She put her chin in the air and glanced at him defiantly. 'Kevin badly needed human contact just then and I felt it was my job to supply it.'

'There's no need to glare at me like that,' Justin said. 'I think you were quite right.'

Paula's expression changed to one of astonishment. 'But I thought you were on Miss Wallace's side? You told me I should have fetched Sister.'

'For your own sake only. From the patient's point of view you couldn't have been faulted.'

'Thank you.' She was delighted at his praise. 'Poor Kevin—I felt so terribly sorry for him. Did you know he and Jean were going to be married?'

'Yes. His parents told me.'

They sat in silence for a moment, staring at the

lake but not really seeing the antics of the water-fowl. Then Justin roused himself.

'Kevin's very young—only twenty. He'll get over it in time. Perhaps even quite quickly. It's Jean's parents I'm most sorry for. They'll have the memory of the tragedy with them for the rest of their lives.'

The surface of the water rippled and blurred suddenly as Paula's eyes filled with tears. She brushed them away. impatiently, hoping Justin hadn't noticed, and stood up.

'I think I've been lazy long enough. I'll walk back to the hospital and see if anybody will play tennis. Have you decided how you're going to spend the rest of your free day?'

There was a brief pause before he answered and then he said casually, 'Only the last part of it. Are you off duty at eight?'

'Thereabouts.' Startled, her pulses quickening a little, she looked down at him. 'Why?'

'Because I think it would be a good idea to drive out of London and have a drink and some food somewhere in the country. It wouldn't be much fun alone, though, so will you come with me?'

'Oh!' Her colour deepened slightly. 'Well—thanks. I'd like that very much.'

'Good.' Justin smiled at her, his eyes alight with pleasure. 'I'll look out for you as soon after eight as you can manage.'

Paula returned to St Andrews at such a pace that

she arrived much too hot to contemplate tennis. Why on earth hadn't she stayed sitting under the tree with Justin where it was cool? Her reason for making the first move to leave had been a complex one and she had regretted it almost at once when he issued his surprising invitation.

She spent the rest of the morning trying to study but she wasn't very successful because every few minutes she had to drag her thoughts back from a joyous contemplation of the evening.

She was nervous when she went into Kevin's room but she found him quiet and listless, his storm of emotion all expended. There was a new patient in the ward, a man with severe breathing difficulties who needed constant care, and the afternoon and early evening passed at a good pace.

Justin was near the main gate. He saw Paula approaching in the mirror and leapt out of his car to greet her.

'Will you be warm enough?' he asked. 'I could put the roof up in a few minutes.'

'I'll be okay. I've brought an anorak as well as a sweater, since it seems to have turned cooler. It's such a thrill to drive in an open car so please don't spoil it.'

'Do you drive?' He turned the ignition key and the engine roared into life. 'If so, I'd be happy to let you have a go when we get out of London.'

'*No!*' The violence of her refusal astonished him and he turned his head to glance at her.

'That rather sounds as though you can drive but don't want to for some reason,' he suggested.

She hadn't expected such perception and was momentarily at a loss for words. 'I used to drive,' she admitted at last, 'but I never had much chance to practise after I passed my test and—and—' She came to a full stop.

Justin waited and then asked, 'And what? Or don't you want to tell me?'

'I don't want to but I think I will, all the same. I want you to understand why I won't drive your car—or any other, ever.'

She paused to sort out her thoughts and then began to speak in a slow and hesitant way.

'You've heard me mention the accident I was involved in but I've never told you the whole truth—that I was the driver. It happened after a party and my friends had had too much to drink. I drink very little and I was quite sober—I even passed the breathalyser test—and so I didn't have any option about driving.'

'So what caused the accident?'

'It was a frosty night. We went into a skid and I didn't have the experience to control it.' Paula broke off to swallow. 'My boy friend was very badly injured and he died later—quite a while later—in the ICU at the local hospital. I felt it was all my fault and I was very upset.'

'You told me about the life-support machine being switched off,' Justin said gently. 'It was a terrible time for you but it's over now. I hope very much that you've reached the point where you can put it behind you.'

Paula thought about it. If she was honest she must admit that she was recovering from the experience. She would never forget it, probably never cease to be influenced by it, but it no longer lay over her like a menacing black cloud, casting a shadow over everything that she did.

'I think I put it behind me when I failed my SRN exam. I knew then that I'd got to stop thinking about the past and get my future into some sort of order. I believed I was managing it pretty well until the scene with Kevin set me back a bit where Miss Wallace is concerned.'

'She'll get over it, and so will you.' Justin touched her hand briefly with his fingers. 'I would say you were doing very well indeed.'

'Thanks.' Paula was pleased and touched by his praise.

'No more secrets?' he asked lightly.

'No more.'

He said something in reply but the rushing wind made it inaudible. It couldn't possibly have been 'How lucky you are!'—or could it? Paula stole a glance at his profile, outlined against a grey-blue sky, but it told her nothing except that his mouth was rather grimly set.

They were already beginning to shake off the sprawling tentacles of London and patches of green became ever more frequent. Justin obviously knew exactly where he was going and, when they reached the real country, he drove confidently down narrow roads and through villages fringed with executive-type houses.

Eventually he drew up at an inn with diamond-paned windows and a roof covered with mossy tiles. Virginia creeper clambered up the walls and geraniums blazed in tubs along the front.

'It's been tarted up quite a bit but it's basically the real thing,' he said. 'Not like that phoney place at Seagate.'

'It's very attractive,' Paula agreed as she led the way into the pretty old-world bar.

The room was full of affluent-looking men and women, the latter mostly thin and wearing smartly cut slacks, whereas their husbands tended to be overweight even when still quite young. They stood talking in groups and Paula chose a seat as far from them as possible.

As Justin went to order their food and drinks she was swept by a wild crazy longing for the sweet salt-scented air of Seagate, the rough grassy bank and the wonderful intimacy of the tiny world they had occupied there—just the two of them.

Perhaps it was due to the sophisticated surroundings but, as they ate and drank, conversation became more and more difficult. Afterwards Paula could remember nothing of what they had talked about, only that she had been filled with a strange sort of uneasiness.

Was it premonition? She neither knew nor cared. The only thing which really mattered happened on the way home.

Justin drove slowly, almost as though he were looking for something. When he found a quiet country road with wide grass verges and overhanging trees, he slowed down even more.

As the car halted beneath a spreading oak tree, Paula's heart began to beat so fast she could hardly breathe. They were as much alone here as they had been at Seagate and Justin must be as aware of it as she was.

With a low murmur which sounded like 'Paula—oh, Paula darling—' he took her into his arms.

She closed her eyes and her body nestled against his, fitting there so neatly it seemed as though they must belong together. With a sigh of sheer physical pleasure she surrendered to the rapture of a long, long kiss. It was just as it had been before only—so it seemed—with a deeper meaning, a greater intensity, a more certain awareness of loving and being loved.

But after a while Justin stirred. He lifted his head and she saw beads of sweat on his forehead.

He said, with a sort of groan, 'Oh God—I never meant this to happen. I was going to be so controlled and sensible. But somehow I didn't seem able to help myself.'

It was like a slap in the face. Bewildered and hurt, Paula straightened up and turned to stare at him.

'I don't understand. Why does it matter that you didn't mean it to happen? It *has* happened and that seems to me to be the important thing.' Her eyes, wide and anxious, gazed into his.

Justin flung her an anguished glance and then looked away. 'It's important all right but it shouldn't be. I ought never to have taken you to Seagate—that's where it all began. And when we came out this evening I intended to try and put things right. There's nowhere you can talk privately at the hospital. I thought—out here, in the country—I could maybe straighten it all out.'

Cold sick dread caught Paula by the throat. She choked and only with a immense effort regained a measure of composure.

She said in a small frightened voice, 'You're still talking in riddles. I'm trying very hard to understand but I can't make any sense out of it at all.'

'I'm not surprised,' Justin told her bitterly. 'I don't quite understand myself but I've got to make an attempt to explain it to you.' He took her hand and intertwined his fingers with hers.

'Do you mind if I speak quite frankly, Paula? I don't want to say anything which will upset you and yet—'

'Go right ahead,' she interrupted. 'And don't bother about my feelings. I'd far rather be told the truth—whatever it is—than be fobbed off with vague statements which mean nothing at all. Which is what it seems to me you've been doing so far.'

'I deserved that,' he said quietly. 'In fact I deserve every harsh thing you can think up to say about me.'

Paula looked at him stonily. 'Please get on with it. I'm listening.'

Justin was having difficulty in speaking. He swallowed painfully and somehow found his voice.

'Here goes then. I was attracted to you almost from the beginning. I didn't let it bother me because—well, a man often sees some girl or other who appeals to him but it's of no importance in his life. He admires her looks, or her personality, but it goes no farther than that and she's almost immediately forgotten. That's how it should have been with you, but I couldn't forget you because we were always meeting.'

He paused, as though expecting a comment, but Paula remained silent and after a moment he continued speaking.

'After that things got out of hand. I make no excuses for myself. I know I've behaved abominably and all I can hope for is that I haven't done any harm. Please, Paula darling—tell me it doesn't matter. Or even that you hate me, if you like.'

He mustn't be allowed to guess how greatly it mattered. However much her heart suffered, her pride must be allowed to remain intact.

She said bitterly, her voice little more than a whisper, 'I shall certainly do my best to hate you, for a little while anyway.' Her voice strengthened. 'But you mustn't imagine you've broken my heart—or even dented it. We had fun together and it was nice while it lasted, but the thing I shall miss most is riding in this gorgeous car. Possessing a vehicle like this really does give you a most unfair advantage where girls are concerned.'

'Bless you, Paula—I knew you'd understand.' Justin gave her hand a final squeeze and released it. 'No hard feelings then?'

'Not serious ones. Just resentment at being made use of.'

'I'm sorry,' he said wretchedly. 'And also very grateful to you for being so nice about it. I was very much afraid that the—the affair might mean more to you than I wanted it to.'

'You flatter yourself!' Her lips curled with genuine scorn.

Justin looked at her silently, and when she saw the distress in his eyes she wished passionately— just for a moment—that she hadn't taken up this don't-care attitude, that she had been truthful and told him exactly what he had done to her.

CHAPTER SEVEN

SHE wouldn't be able to keep it up much longer—Paula knew that for sure. 'I think you'd better take me back to St Andrews,' she said, her voice almost giving her away.

'First tell me I'm forgiven or I shall feel even worse about it than I do already,' Justin begged.

She shrugged and half turned her back on him. 'I don't care how badly you feel. I've no intention of pretending. At this moment I don't feel in the mood for forgiveness but maybe I'll get around to it in due course. When I reach that stage I'll let you know.'

He made no attempt to argue and they drove back to Belton Park in total silence. Fortunately it was dark now and there was no danger Justin would notice the large tear which occasionally rolled down Paula's face in spite of all her efforts.

When they reached the hospital she jumped out of the car almost before it had stopped. She just managed a choked 'Goodnight' before fleeing to her room.

She could weep there in that blessed privacy, weep until she had no more tears to shed. And then, lying sleepless in the darkness, struggle to put together again the pieces of her life so that she could go on duty in the morning without giving her secret away to anyone.

Least of all Justin.

It wasn't easy to keep her misery hidden from the public gaze. Discreetly applied make-up covered up all signs of distress as far as her appearance was concerned, but she was unhappily aware that her manner was unnaturally subdued.

Kevin noticed at once.

'What's wrong with you this morning? You've hardly said a word.'

'I've got a headache.'

Paula had snatched at the excuse, unoriginal as it was, but she immediately felt ashamed because he had had so much more to bear than herself.

Somehow she conjured up a smile. 'Don't take any notice of me. It's not just the headache. I'm in a thoroughly bad mood.'

Kevin glanced through the open door, from which he could see part of the ward.

'I don't wonder this sort of work gets you down sometimes. Do you ever feel you'd like to chuck it up and do something else?'

Startled, she looked at him for a moment without speaking. Would that perhaps be the solution? To give up nursing? Abandon the fight to reinstate herself in the eyes of authority and find some less demanding job?

'I feel like that right now,' she said frankly.

To her surprise he reached out and caught her

hand. 'You mustn't say things like that! You're far too good a nurse to dream of giving up. But, just in case you did mean it, please don't go yet awhile. I couldn't bear it here without you. I looked for you yesterday morning and you weren't on duty, and then in the afternoon you were so busy I scarcely saw you.'

Perhaps it would have been sensible to tell him why she had kept away, that it had been because emotional links between a nurse and her patient were frowned on, but she couldn't do it. His blue eyes were imploring her to understand his need of her, not to let him down.

And so, instead of returning his hand gently to where it had lain on the bedspread, she took it in both her own and held it warmly.

'I wouldn't be allowed to leave until I'd worked out my notice, Kevin, so I shall certainly still be here as long as you're hospitalised. But I expect they'll let you go home before long. Have the doctors said anything about it?'

He shook his head. 'I haven't seen the specialist since I got my memory back.'

With an effort Paula recalled which day of the week it was. 'Mr Browning is due tomorrow. I expect he'll tell you when you're likely to be discharged.'

The tall thin consultant in neurology arrived late the following morning. He brought an imposing team from West City with him and was also attended by the RSO at St Andrews, Justin and Tony.

Inevitably the informal atmosphere of the ward vanished during his visits. Beds were in neat rows, with castors all pointing the same way, and the flowers were kept strictly to their appointed places. Beneath her elegant lace-trimmed cap Sister's curls were lacquered firmly into order.

During the great man's tour the nurses kept carefully out of the way, so that Paula had no means of knowing what he said to Kevin. But afterwards, when they were serving lunch to the few patients capable of eating it in the normal way, she went to his room and asked him.

'He said I could go home next week—about Wednesday if the doctors here are satisfied with my general condition. But I've got to attend his clinic at West City.' His voice was flat and uninterested.

'You'll be glad to get away from here,' Paula encouraged him. 'The ICU is a depressing place and there's no need for you to be here any longer. You don't really need nursing, only general taking care of.'

'I shall miss having everything done for me,' he said wistfully. 'I don't feel at all independent.'

'You soon will,' she assured him, 'when you get home. And I expect Sister will try and get you rehabilitated during the few days you've got left with us.'

But Kevin refused to cheer up. 'I'm dreading it,'

he confessed. 'While I'm here I don't have to face up to the fact that Jean's dead. It'll be different at home.'

Paula could think of nothing to say so she just stayed there, holding his hand and trying to give comfort by the mere fact of human contact.

She was still there, a few minutes later, when Sister looked in.

'I couldn't think where you'd got to, Paula.' Anne glanced at the linked hands and tightened her lips. 'You're urgently needed in the ward.'

Her tone had been sharp and her expression unsympathetic, most unusual with her. Paula noted both manifestations of disapproval and knew she should be concerned about them. No doubt Miss Wallace had requested that a watch should be kept on her behaviour but somehow it no longer seemed to matter.

'I'm just coming,' she said composedly, giving Kevin a strained smile before releasing herself.

The following Wednesday Justin confirmed that he was well enough to be discharged, and Paula went to the office to ring up his mother and ask her to arrange for him to be fetched that afternoon.

'We were expecting it, of course, after what the specialist said, but it's marvellous to have it confirmed,' Mrs Blake said, her voice quivering with emotion. 'If only poor Jean had been as fortunate! I'm afraid Kevin's going to miss her terribly, much more than he's done in hospital.'

She broke off to regain composure and then continued in a worried tone, 'I'm just a little bit anxious about looking after him. Will he need any special care?'

'Oh no, nothing out of the ordinary—breakfast in bed and that sort of thing. It's very important he shouldn't get overtired.'

'Kevin's very difficult to handle sometimes. I'm sure he'll think I'm fussing. Will you have a word with him before he leaves, Nurse?'

She promised to do so, and seized her opportunity when she was doing Kevin's packing for him.

'You've been a very good patient while you've been here. Just try and keep it up when you're at home, and don't try to do too much. I've told your mother you'll have to be sensible and take it easy.'

'I'm sure I'd be good if you were there to boss me instead of Mum.' His thin face was illuminated by a smile. 'Wouldn't it be great if the hospital sent you home with me as a special nurse! Is there any chance of it?'

'Of course not.' Paula laughed. 'For one thing I'm a hospital nurse and not a private one, and you don't need any special care anyway.'

'Couldn't you pop in and see me during your off duty time? I live in Belton Park, not far from the hospital, so it wouldn't be much trouble.'

She hesitated, suddenly very tempted to fall in with his suggestion, not because she really thought it was a good idea but because it seemed wonderful to be so much wanted.

'I suppose I could but it wouldn't be until next week because I've got a free weekend and I'm going home on Saturday.'

'Oh.' He was obviously disappointed. 'Where do you live?'

'The other side of London. Too far to come visiting around here.'

He sat in silence for a moment, watching her as she turned out his locker, and then his face lit up.

'I've just had a super idea! Why don't you come and stay at our house for the weekend? Or are you doing anything special at your home you don't want to miss?'

Paula sat back on her heels and looked at him, considerably startled by the suggestion.

'I wasn't doing anything very much, only taking the dog for walks and having a lazy time generally. Were you really serious?'

'Of course I was.' Kevin was radiant because she hadn't turned down the idea at once.

'But what about your mother?'

'She'd be delighted to have you and we've bags of room. There's a spare bedroom which is always kept ready.' A flicker of pain crossed his face. 'Jean used to stay there sometimes.'

Paula stared absently down at the pyjamas she was folding. She liked Kevin and was sorry for him. There was no reason in the world why she shouldn't accept the invitation. Her parents, who saw her fairly frequently, wouldn't argue about her change of plan.

'Okay,' she said abruptly. 'I'd like to come if that's what you really want.'

His pleasure in her acceptance was heart-warming and she arranged to arrive on Saturday morning. Discovering that the distance was not too great for walking she listened carefully to his directions and memorised them.

Saturday was cool and cloudy, with a threat of rain. By the time Paula started out the first few drops were falling and she knew it would be more sensible to take a taxi.

As she hesitated at the entrance to St Andrews, aware that she couldn't really afford it so near the end of the month, a voice spoke suddenly from behind her.

'Would you like a lift to the station? I'm going to the Post Office and could easily drop you there.'

Justin stood there, tall and remote-looking, his face wearing a careful expression of polite concern.

'No thanks.' Paula's refusal was instinctive. She stopped staring up at the sky and took a step forward. 'I don't think it's going to rain much and I like walking.'

'Even carrying a suitcase?'

'It's not heavy.'

Justin glanced at the lowering sky and the rain

chose that moment to change from a slight drizzle to a much more purposeful descent.

'I know you'd rather get soaked than accept a lift from me,' he said tautly, 'but I'm not going to let you be such a fool. It's obviously intending to pour.'

He snatched at her arm and began marching her rapidly towards where his car was parked. Furious, she tried to drag herself free but his grip tightened to a band of steel and she was powerless.

'How dare you treat me like this!' she flung at him angrily.

'I told you. I'm not letting you tramp all the way to the station in a downpour.'

The hospital drive was far from deserted. Night nurses were hurrying across to the Home and doctors going to and from the Residency. There were also a few members of the public who had some reason or other for being there.

Paula gritted her teeth and ceased her resistance. She couldn't make a scene here, that was for sure. In an icy silence she watched Justin struggling with the hood of his car.

But as they drove out into the road she was obliged to speak.

'I'm not going to the station.'

'Not?' She had obviously surprised him. 'Then where?'

'I'm spending the weekend with—with friends. No 24 Parkside Avenue.' She glanced quickly sideways to see if the address meant anything to him. It obviously didn't and she added with cold politeness, 'I'm afraid it's out of your way but there's no need to take me right to the house. I can easily walk the last part.'

'I thought the object of this exercise was to save you getting wet.' Justin thrust out his jaw and glared at some children who were threatening to run across in front of them. 'I'll take you all the way.'

Paula gave up the argument. After all, what did it matter? Kevin wouldn't be up yet so there was no danger he would be watching out for her. As they turned into Parkside Avenue, a long straight road very pleasantly lined with trees, she began to look for No 24.

They found it quite soon, a semi-detached house with a pretty front garden and discreet net curtains. There was no sign of life and Paula got out quickly and with relief when Justin stopped at the gate.

'Thanks for the lift.' Without looking at him she banged the car door shut and turned towards the house.

And at that moment the front door opened and Kevin's mother came out into the porch, beaming a welcome.

'Lovely to see you, Paula dear! Kevin's been practically counting the minutes.'

'Good God!' Justin's astonished comment

reached Paula clearly. 'That's Mrs Blake. What on earth is all this about?'

There was just time for Paula to answer him before she advanced to meet her hostess.

'I told you I was going to stay with friends, didn't I?'

Let him make what he could of that, she thought defiantly, and then did her best to shake off the effects of the unfortunate beginning to the weekend.

'Now I don't want you to imagine you're here to work, dear,' Mrs Blake was saying. 'I know this is your free weekend and you need a good rest. It's just that Kevin seems to think such a lot of you and there's no doubt you've helped him through a very difficult time. His Dad and I will always be grateful to you.'

'How is he?' Paula asked. 'Kevin, I mean, of course.'

'He's not sleeping very well. Says his bed feels unfamiliar, the silly boy. I would have thought he would appreciate it after that hard hospital bed. Come along upstairs and I'll show you your room.'

It was at the back, overlooking the garden, and very attractively furnished in a feminine sort of way.

'This was my daughter's room before she married,' Mrs Blake said. 'Do you want to unpack or shall I take you straight to see Kevin?'

'I can unpack any time.' Paula put down her

suitcase and began to unbutton her raincoat. 'It's a pity it's so wet. I hoped he'd be able to sit in the garden.'

'The weather man says it'll clear up later on and the patio will soon dry. Are you ready, dear? Come along then.'

Kevin's room was next door. He was sitting up in bed, looking pale and tired, but his eyes were bright and he was smiling brilliantly. Paula would have liked to count his pulse but she restrained herself.

'So you actually made it!' was his greeting. 'I was afraid something might crop up to stop you. Did you get very wet?'

She explained briefly that she had had a lift. They talked for a while and then Kevin announced his intention of getting up.

'Do you want any help?' Paula asked, a nurse again for the moment.

He shook his head. 'I can manage okay. See you downstairs.'

He was exhausted when he arrived and obliged to sink into a chair. 'I feel a hundred,' he complained, wiping the sweat of weakness from his forehead.

'I expect you do,' Paula said cheerfully, 'but tomorrow you'll only feel ninety, and after that your age will decrease rapidly until you reach—what is it? Twenty-two?'

'That's right, but I can't imagine it ever happening.'

By lunchtime the sun was shining and they were able to go outside after they had eaten. Stretched out in a long chair, with Kevin half asleep beside her, Paula struggled with a sense of unreality.

What was she doing here, staying with these people who were almost strangers? Even Kevin, whom she had known so intimately at the hospital, had changed in some subtle way. No longer a patient, he was on the verge of becoming—what?'

Paula opened her eyes and stared unseeing at the distant figure of Mr Blake busy among his vegetables.

All her instincts told her that Kevin was in danger of forming a romantic attachment to herself. On the rebound from Jean, he was very vulnerable and—given the slightest encouragement—would undoubtedly take the first step towards falling in love with his ex-nurse.

It mustn't be allowed to happen. No matter how pleasant she found his devotion, or how much it soothed her sore heart, she must somehow hold it in check.

At first she found it quite easy. Kevin was very tired and content just to be at home again and to enjoy her company. But on Sunday morning his parents went to church and he took advantage of his mother's absence to announce his intention of taking a short walk in the park.

'You're not ready for that,' Paula said flatly.

'I feel fine this morning. I'm sure I could manage a short distance.'

He was so determined that she gave in, walking very slowly at his side and keeping a sharp look-out in case his weakness should cause him to stumble. Before long he was obliged to admit himself beaten and she had to help him return to the house.

'You *must* remember that you had a very serious accident and were in bed for a long time,' she scolded. 'You won't get over the effects of it completely for months.'

'I thought you were supposed to be cheering me up,' Kevin protested.

'I don't believe in not facing up to facts.'

'I suppose you're right.' He sighed heavily and was silent for a moment. 'It's a funny thing,' he continued hesitantly, 'but Jean no longer seems real to me. It makes me feel so ashamed and yet I honestly can't help it.'

'I'm sure there's no need to feel ashamed. These things happen and people can't control the way they feel about other people.'

Or she wouldn't be in love with Justin, Paula added bitterly in her own mind. There was no happiness in it and no hope either. She would be far better off without it.

'I should stop worrying about Jean if I were you,' she said aloud. 'She would almost certainly want you to pick up the pieces and make a fresh start.'

'Yes, I think she would. She was a great girl

and—and—' He broke off and swallowed.

Intending only to show sympathy Paula laid her hand on his arm. They were sitting side-by-side on the settee, with a very sensible distance between them. But suddenly Kevin moved nearer and leaned forward to look into her face.

'Will you help me mend my shattered life, Paula?' he implored her. 'Will you let me go on seeing you—please!'

And with an abruptness which gave no opportunity for protest, he kissed her violently on the lips.

CHAPTER EIGHT

TAKEN completely by surprise Paula remained passive for a moment, neither responding to the kiss nor attempting to evade it. Then, as gently as she could, she disengaged herself and moved farther away.

Kevin looked at her reproachfully. 'Are you angry with me? I'm sorry if that's the case because I would do it again if I got the chance.'

'Then I'd better take care you *don't* get the chance!' She spoke lightly but there was an underlying seriousness in her voice.

He immediately looked hurt and she wished she hadn't answered him so frankly. He was still very much an invalid, she reminded herself, with his emotions barely under control, and it was more than likely he would do and say things he would regret later.

'Listen, love—' She spoke quietly and affectionately, hoping to strike just the right note. 'It honestly wouldn't be a good idea to get involved with me or anyone else just now. You need time to recover from the awful experience you've passed through, and it's your *friends* who will help you best simply because they're not too close to you emotionally.

She was talking like some sort of psychiatric

adviser and she was a year younger than Kevin. Paula broke off to smile ruefully at herself and found him scowling at the floor, his sensitive mouth set in a mutinous line.

'That's a load of rubbish,' he told her flatly. 'At the moment I couldn't care less about my friends. They don't know anything about the way I feel just now and when they visited me in hospital I could tell they were embarrassed. But you *do* understand—partly because you're a nurse, I suppose, but mostly because you're kind and sympathetic and—and on my wavelength.'

It was impossible not to be warmed and flattered by his estimate of her. Impossible, too, not to feel glad because somebody wanted her, even though the person who mattered most had made it very plain he didn't.

'You're very sweet to view me like that,' she said a little shakily. 'I don't deserve it a bit but I like hearing it.'

'Then will you agree to let me go on seeing you?' Kevin asked eagerly. 'You won't let this weekend be just a one-off occasion?'

'I shall certainly want to know how your convalescence is progressing. And I'd very much like to come and see you sometimes. It will be nice to have a home in Belton Park where I can call in now and then.'

'Not now and then,' he said at once. 'I want you to come often.'

Paula hesitated, uncertain how to deal with that, and she was relieved to hear the front door opening as Mr and Mrs Blake returned from church. This enabled her to get away with a noncommittal smile which Kevin was obliged to accept without argument.

The rest of the day passed peacefully and pleasantly. Rested and refreshed, mentally as well as physically, Paula returned to the hospital. It had been a successful weekend, on the whole.

When she went on duty in the morning it seemed as though she had been away much longer than a couple of days. There were three new patients, two men and a girl, all with head injuries incurred in the same accident. The girl reminded her a little of Jean and momentarily her thoughts flew to Kevin's attachment to herself.

He would get over it soon, of course. It was almost certainly only a manifestation of convalescence.

And if he didn't? But Paula refused to contemplate that.

Later that morning she was returning from her coffee break and taking the short cut across the garden, when she saw ahead of her a tall slim girl in a doctor's white coat. She had auburn hair neatly tied back with a black ribbon and held herself superbly and walked like a model.

She obviously knew her way about for she took the path through the flower beds which led to the

Residency and disappeared inside without hesitation. No stranger, apparently—but who on earth was she?

Interested because of the girl's striking appearance, Paula took the first opportunity of asking for information.

'Sounds like the lovely Liz—Dr Elizabeth Deben,' Sally told her. 'I heard she was back.'

'Back from where?'

'The States. She's been away two months or so on a sort of busman's holiday.'

'But who *is* she?' Paula persisted. 'Is she on the staff here?'

'That's right. She's a registrar attached to the RSO. She'd been here quite a short time when she got this super chance of going to America and the hospital agreed to release her temporarily. She caused quite a stir when she first came here, I can tell you. The men all went down before her like ninepins. With those sort of looks you can't wonder at it.'

'So what happened?'

'She looked them over, discarded all the mere housemen and then picked out one of the others as her regular escort.'

Perhaps she should have guessed earlier but not until that moment did Paula realise what was coming. Half turning her back and stirring vigorously at the milky drink she was mixing, she asked a careless question over her shoulder.

'Who was the lucky guy?'

'Justin Stewart.' Sally paused to break an egg into a glass. 'At least I suppose he considers himself lucky. They're two of a kind anyway—both walk around as though they owned the place, so busy playing it cool they don't have time to be human. Not that they aren't very good doctors, of course, and I'd give Justin at any rate full marks for the way he treats the patients. Liz is a bit inclined to talk down to them.'

Paula gave the milk a last stir. She must say something or Sally would think it odd.

'Thanks for putting me in the picture. In a small place like this you need to know who everybody is.'

Carrying the glass with exaggerated care, she went back to the ward. As she walked slowly towards the convalescent patient who awaited her, the pieces of the jigsaw fell inexorably into place.

Liz Deben was the reason why Justin had behaved so strangely. Very likely he really had been briefly attracted to her—Paula—but he had quickly got a grip on himself. In any case it wouldn't have lasted five minutes after Liz came back. One glance at that lovely face and long slim legs and he wouldn't remember Paula existed.

But *why*, her heart cried out in anguish, hadn't he told her about Liz?

Suddenly she realised that he had—right at the

beginning and in a very vague sort of way. When he asked her to go with him to his cousin's party he'd said something about being temporarily without a partner. Paula hadn't taken much notice at the time but she now understood only too well.

Somehow she managed to put it out of her mind and concentrate on work. But at lunchtime she saw Justin and Liz walking together towards the doctors' dining room. The girl was talking animatedly, no doubt about her experiences in the States, and Justin was listening with his head slightly bent and an absorbed expression on his face.

No doubt he was finding it all intensely interesting, Paula thought bitterly. And it would be all the more fascinating when told to him by a beautiful girl whom he loved.

That afternoon Liz came to the Unit, unfortunately choosing a time when Paula was in charge. There was no way she could avoid the glamorous doctor who—because of her long absence—was unfamiliar with most of the patients and therefore asked a lot of questions.

'I can remember a few of the people who were here when I left,' she said in her clear cool voice. 'Martin, for instance. What happened to him?'

'He died.'

'I was afraid he would. There was really very little hope.' Much taller than Paula, she looked down at her with polite curiosity. 'You're new since I went away. What's your name?'

Paula supplied the information curtly and then felt strangely impelled to add to it.

'I was transferred here from West City. I've only got another three weeks in the Unit, thank goodness.'

'You don't like it?'

She hesitated, aware that her actual dislike of the Unit had faded and her urgent wish was to get moved to a medical ward where she would no longer see Justin—and Liz. But the long-lashed greenish eyes were looking at her intently and she thought she saw disapproval in them. Because of that she answered sharply, voicing the opinion she had held when she first came to St Andrews.

'I certainly prefer wards which don't have an invisible notice over the door "Abandon hope all ye who enter here".'

'But that's ridiculous!' Liz sounded thoroughly put out. 'This ward is full of hope. Else why would we keep on with all these life-support machines? You must have had some patients who made complete recoveries since you came here.'

'Well—yes, some,' Paula agreed.

'There you are then! You've been proved wrong by your own words. And I hope you won't go around saying what you've just said to me. It's most important that people shouldn't get the idea this ward is full of terminal cases.'

Paula closed her lips tightly and remained silent. She had absolutely no intention of doing what she had just been warned against, but she couldn't bring herself to say so.

Liz waited a moment, shrugged and then said icily, 'Perhaps you will now take me round the beds and supply me with all the information you can about each patient.'

That at least Paula could accomplish efficiently and she immediately assumed a professional mask and gave her full attention to the task. Liz asked a great many questions and appeared satisfied with the answers. Her guide was obliged to admit that she had a quick and receptive mind.

She went away at last and Paula relaxed, but before long she had another visitor. This time it was Tony.

'Hi, Paula!' He was, as always, cheerful and schoolboyish. 'How are things?'

'Much as usual. Did you come to see anybody in particular?'

'I came to see you—got an invitation for you. Will you come to a party with me on Saturday night?'

Her first instinct was to refuse but then she hesitated. After all—why not? She liked Tony and thought it probable that his amorous intentions would be easier to handle at a social occasion than in the darkness and seclusion of the back row at the cinema.

'Okay,' she agreed. 'Who's giving this party and where's it to be held?'

'At the Residency—and we're all giving it. The doctors who live there, I mean. It's to welcome Liz Deben back from the States.'

'What?' Appalled, Paula gazed at him in dismay and tried to think of some excuse for withdrawing her acceptance.

'What's wrong?' Tony asked in surprise. 'You're looking most peculiar.'

No flash of inspiration had come to Paula's rescue and she was obliged to stammer incoherently. 'N-nothing. Except that I hadn't realised her return was of such importance it needed a party to celebrate it.'

'You've seen her, haven't you?' Tony demanded.

'Yes, but—'

'Then you shouldn't ask silly questions. It's not only that she's so decorative to look at but everybody likes her. She's a really nice girl.'

'I'll take your word for it,' Paula said lightly.

She was committed to it now and nothing short of illness could save her. For a while she was tempted to feign sudden illness on Saturday but pride came to her rescue. She'd go through with it if it killed her, and by so doing she would show Justin once and for all that he meant as little to her as she obviously did to him.

The Residency was a large square building of red brick, once the home of a wealthy Edwardian businessman. It now consisted of bedsittingrooms and flatlets, with a communal lounge. Most of the housemen and registrars lived there, even those who were married.

When Paula and Tony arrived the big room was already half full. People were still at the stage of standing about and holding drinks as they talked in small groups. Liz, looking dramatically beautiful in black-and-white, greeted them gaily and surprised Paula by remembering her name.

'Help yourselves.'

She waved her hand towards a generously loaded table and they did as they had been told, loading their plates with cheese and french bread, and then carrying food and glasses to a corner and surveying the scene.

'It doesn't seem to have warmed up much yet,' Tony said. 'I hope it gets going before I have to leave. Did you know I was on call?'

'You didn't mention it, but I don't know why you should take it for granted you'll be called out.'

Paula had answered him absently. She was surreptitiously looking round the room for Justin but he didn't seem to have arrived yet.

When he did come in his arrival was so unobtrusive that at first she didn't notice him. She was dancing with Tony to a slow languorous tune. He held her tightly, his cheek against hers. In view of the impression she wanted to give it could hardly have been a better moment for Justin to pass them with Liz.

Paula should have felt triumphant but instead her feeling was only of pain, pain because he was with Liz and not with herself, pain because of the deception she was practising by pretending Tony meant anything to her. It was a pain so great that not merely her heart but her whole body seemed to ache with it.

Because of it she was extra gay, laughing at Tony's feeblest jokes, working so hard at giving an impression of a girl having a thoroughly good time that after a while he looked curiously at her.

'If it weren't for my certain knowledge that you've only had two glasses of wine I'd say you were a bit the worse for wear, Paula.'

'The worse for wear! What a disgusting way of putting it,' she mocked.

'Well, you know what I mean.' His arm tightened about her. 'How about coming outside to cool off?'

'No, thanks,' she said quickly.

Tony looked down at her and raised one eyebrow. 'If I remember rightly you weren't very cooperative when we went to the cinema. Don't I appeal to you?'

'Not in that way, Tony dear.' To soften it she rubbed her head against his shoulder affectionately. 'But I like you a lot in spite of the way you terrified me when you pretended to be a ghost.'

'Why drag that up? It was ages ago, anyway—I'm a reformed character now. I haven't got locked in the Nurses' Home since that night when you let me climb out of your window.'

'I didn't exactly *let* you—' Paula broke off as his bleeper sounded almost in her ear.

'To hell with it!' Tony disengaged himself. 'Afraid I'll have to leave you, love, and make for the nearest phone.'

Abandoned, Paula sat watching the dancing, hoping that Tony would soon come back. But he only looked in to say that an emergency had cropped up in one of the surgical wards and he didn't know how long he would be.

She looked at her watch. 'It's getting quite late. If you're not back in about fifteen minutes I think I'll leave. I'm on early duty in the morning.'

Conscientiously she waited the full time and then began to edge her way towards the door. She supposed she ought to thank somebody for the party but the senior doctors had already left with their wives and nobody would notice if she just crept away.

Liz certainly wouldn't. She was the centre of an animated group, all discussing something with great vigour. Strangely enough, Justin wasn't one of them and Paula wondered if he had also been called over to the hospital.

But when she reached the front door and was just stepping outside, a figure suddenly loomed up out of the darkness. Considerably startled, Paula stifled a scream and then saw that it was Justin.

'Sorry if I startled you,' he said. 'It was terribly hot in there and I felt an urge for fresh air. What's happened to Tony?'

'He got bleeped.'

'I see. Then I'd better escort you across the grounds instead,' Justin said coolly.

'*No!*' Paula struggled for composure. 'I mean— there isn't the slightest need for me to have an escort.'

'I disagree.'

He set out at a leisurely pace and she had no choice but to accompany him, since to remain standing on the doorstep would have looked absurd.

As she walked at his side she could hardly believe it was happening. When she had arrived at the party with Tony, she would never have believed it possible that she might leave with Justin. And yet, there they were, strolling along together in a silence so absolute that to break it was rapidly becoming of supreme importance.

She could think of nothing to say; her tongue felt as rigid as her limbs. All around them the garden lay quietly in the darkness, barely lit by a dying moon festooned in clouds. There was a faint hum of distant traffic but otherwise nothing disturbed the peace.

It could have been so perfect but Paula was conscious of nothing except a terrible longing to put an end to it.

They had almost reached the Nurses' Home before she found her voice.

'There's no need for you to come any farther. I shall be quite safe now.'

Justin halted. In the faint light coming from the doorway she could see his face, devoid of colour, his shadowed eyes giving away nothing of his feeling.'

But there was no lack of emotion in his voice when he said urgently, a hand on her arm, 'Don't go in for a minute, Paula—please. I've got to talk to you. There's so much I want to explain.'

CHAPTER NINE

'IF it's anything like the last so-called explanation you gave me I don't want to hear.' Paula shook off his restraining arm and faced him defiantly. 'But if any clarifying were needed I would only have to look at Liz Deben for everything to fall into place. There's nothing left to be said between you and me. Nothing!'

'I admit I ought to have told you about Liz right at the beginning,' Justin admitted. 'But the fact remains that I didn't and for the very good reason that it didn't seem necessary. Later on, when it really *was* necessary, I still couldn't tell you because it was disastrously too late. You couldn't possibly be expected to understand.'

'Riddles again! You're quite an expert at them, aren't you?' Paula mocked. 'I was never very clever at guessing the answers and in your case I don't intend even to try. If only you'd stop tying yourself in verbal knots it would all be perfectly simple. You have a very glamorous girl friend just back from America. What more do you want?'

Justin did not answer immediately. He was standing very still, his arms at his sides. But suddenly he took a step forward and seized her in an iron grip.

'This is what I want, Paula,' he said quietly.

With a swift movement he bent his head and she felt the full impact of his mouth on her own. It was a fierce demanding kiss which took the breath from her body and set her heart hammering. For a moment she closed her eyes and allowed emotion to sweep over her in a great wave of longing.

And then reaction set in and she brought up both hands and pushed Justin away with such force that he recoiled against the wall. Words poured from her in a torrent of reproach, washing away all the sweetness of the last few seconds.

'I don't know what could possibly have given you the idea you could do that to me! Or do you imagine you can string us both along—Liz and me? If that's the idea, then it's just not on, and I'm sure she'd be the first to agree.'

'If only you'd trust me—'

'Why should I?' she demanded furiously. 'You seem to me to be just about the least trustworthy person I've ever come across.'

That had hurt him. Even in the dim light Paula could see the pain in his face and she experienced a brief crazy gladness because he was suffering too. It was gone in a flash, leaving her empty and cold, drained of emotion, wanting only to be done with this horrible conversation.

'I suppose I deserved that,' Justin said bleakly.

'Yes, I think you did.' Paula turned towards the lighted doorway.

'Wait—' Once more he caught her by the arm. 'I haven't even started to tell you—'

'You've said quite enough. Let me go!' She wrenched herself free. 'I'm not going to listen to any more of your attempts to justify yourself.'

There was anger in Justin's eyes now and he spoke hotly and accusingly. 'You never used to be so unreasonable. I suppose the truth is that you don't want to listen to me. You'd rather listen to Tony, or maybe Kevin Blake. I know he means something in your life. You spent a weekend at his house, didn't you? I drove you there—'

'I didn't ask you for a lift. You practically forced it on me. And I can spend a weekend anywhere I choose without consulting you first. *Goodnight!*'

The last feeble shreds of her anger carried her into the Nurses' Home and down the corridor to her room. But once there she collapsed onto the bed in a torrent of tears. She must have been mad to let Tony persuade her to attend that horrible party. Nothing but the wish to show Justin she didn't care about Liz had made her give in to him.

As a reason for going to a party it was pretty poor, being based merely on pride. Sitting up and scrubbing her face with a sodden handkerchief, Paula doubted very much whether it had worked either. Justin must be well aware by now that she *did* mind about Liz.

She slept at last, to wake early with a headache and in her mind the firm resolution to steer clear in future of all emotional entanglements and concentrate entirely on nursing.

For a few days she was successful and then a phone call from Kevin forced her to face up to the fact that her emotional life was not entirely in her own hands.

'I thought you were coming to see me some time when you were off duty?' he began reproachfully. 'You haven't even rung up to ask how I'm getting on.'

'I'm sorry—I've been terribly busy and I have an awful lot of studying to do in my spare time. But I hadn't forgotten you, Kevin, truly I hadn't.'

'I should hope not! When are you coming round?'

'I'll have to think. But first tell me about yourself. Are you making good progress?'

'I'm doing fine. I can walk halfway round the park now—well, nearly. I'll give you a demonstration when you come and see me. Can we fix a date now?'

'If I can remember when I'm off duty. I think I've got a free afternoon the day after tomorrow. How about that?'

'Does that mean you'll have to go back to the hospital in the evening?' he asked in a disappointed tone.

'Afraid so, but I shall have about three hours off.'

'Then come to lunch. That will make it seem

longer. Please don't refuse, Paula—I shall look forward to it so much.'

She didn't want to hurt him and so she reluctantly agreed to come. In a way it was rewarding to hear the happiness in his voice but she could not feel any more enthusiastic about the invitation.

In actual fact, the occasion turned out to be easy and pleasant. She received a great welcome and was genuinely delighted to find Kevin with a much healthier colour in his thin face. He kissed her quickly, just before his mother appeared, but without the emotional intensity he had displayed before.

'He's so much better,' Mrs Blake told her, 'and a lot of it's due to you, dear. We shall always be grateful.'

Paula went pink with pleasure and spent a quietly happy afternoon in the garden. When Kevin pressed her to come again, she promised at once to do so.

Afterwards she wondered if she wouldn't have been wiser to maintain her previous resistance to Kevin's demands. Wasn't she perhaps making use of this very ordinary 'nice' family to soothe her own sore heart? Was she being quite fair?'

Fortunately she remembered that she would be leaving the ICU quite soon and attending daily at West City for a period of two weeks block study before starting a new ward at St Andrews.

Much as she now wanted to finish with the Unit—

where she was daily obliged to have some contact with Liz and Justin—she was not looking forward to block study. She would be with a set of girls who all knew each other well, and she would be sure to feel herself the odd one out.

On her last day in the ICU Sister called her into the office.

'I've just been writing your report, Paula. I thought you'd like to know that I'm giving you a good one.' She smiled and brushed back her tangle of curls.

'Oh, thank you—' Paula's face lit up with delight. 'I was so afraid that incident with Kevin Blake would have given me a black mark with you as well as Miss Wallace.'

Anne smiled. 'Officially I didn't approve but I'm perfectly well aware that emotional ties can spring into being between a nurse and her patient almost without warning. It's hard for someone your age to know how to handle that sort of situation. As your ward sister I condemned you, but underneath I knew you probably weren't to blame.'

'Miss Wallace tore me off a strip.'

'Of course she did but I expect she understood, nevertheless.'

Paula had serious doubts about this but she kept them to herself. 'Thank you for the report anyway,' she said warmly. 'In a way I shall be sorry to leave the Unit. Do you know where I'm going next?'

'To men's surgical,' Anne said, after consulting a

list. 'You'll probably find it much more interesting and varied than this ward. Head injuries can be very depressing.'

Another surgical ward . . . And she had so much hoped to be sent to a medical department. Paula hastily wiped the dismay from her face, said a polite 'Thank you' and the left the office.

Obviously she would have to continue the hard way to fight her battle against Justin's dominion over her heart.

She said goodbye to the ICU with mixed feelings and in the morning set off in the hospital mini bus for West City Nurse Education Centre, a large old-fashioned house about a mile from the hospital. For a fortnight she gave her full attention to what she was being taught.

The fact that she had done it all before made it much easier. Nevertheless, the test paper at the end of the course was stiff and she was surprised and thrilled to find out she had been placed at the top of the list.

She went home for two nights but returned to Belton Park early on the day before she was to start work in Bradshaw Ward. At a loose end, she felt very tempted to ring up Kevin but restrained herself. Time dragged and she was eager to speed the hours so that she could begin in her new ward and surmount the hurdle of unfamiliar surroundings and a strange sister.

Sister Leyton was very different from Anne

Knox. A thin, harassed-looking woman, she had the pinched look of permanent indigestion and the irritable temper which went with it. But in spite of this, the general opinion at St Andrews was that she ran her ward efficiently and wasn't too bad to work for if you didn't let her ruffle you.

Bradshaw was large and old-fashioned, with the beds rather too close together. It was a busy ward, with a rapid turnover of patients, and Paula was absorbed into it from the moment of her arrival.

Justin came in with Liz and Tony about halfway through the morning. Tony winked at Paula and went off to visit a patient in the side ward, but Liz and Justin remained together.

Both were immaculate in white coats, stethoscopes dangling, their manner suitably grave as they stood one on either side of an operation case which was causing concern.

What a marvellous pair they made, Paula thought bitterly. The man tall, dark-haired and grey-eyed, the girl with her bright hair and brilliant blue eyes. She was tall too, the top of her head well above his shoulder, and they looked so exactly right for each other that Jenny Green, a second year nurse with a romantic outlook, commented on it to Paula.

'Aren't they a super pair! Just think how gorgeous they'll look on their wedding day.'

'Are they officially engaged then?' Paula forced herself to ask.

'People don't always bother with that now, do they? They just get married. But I think it's quite definite. Before she went to America they were always around together and I haven't noticed any difference since she came back, have you?'

'Er—no, but I wasn't here before Liz went away. I didn't know she existed until she suddenly re-appeared.' Her voice quivered a little.

'Nurse Garland!' It was Sister's voice. 'Is it really necessary for me to remind you that there is a great deal to do in this ward?' She turned her attention to Jenny. 'You, too, Nurse Green—how many times have I asked you not to waste time gossiping?'

'I don't know, Sister. Too many, I'm afraid,' Jenny said with a smile which somehow removed the impertinence from her reply.

Sister Leyton snorted and went on her way. Paula was about to do the same when Liz called out to her.

'We would like to examine this patient's wound, Nurse. Will you take the dressing off, please?'

Hastily donning a mask and pulling a trolley with the other hand, Paula joined them and drew the curtains. Justin moved to make room for her, and she squeezed past him with lowered lashes.

Because her hands were trembling a little she was clumsy with the dressing and the man, who had had his gall bladder removed, winced visibly.

Liz said sharply, 'Careful, Nurse! There was no need for that.'

Ignoring the comment, Paula apologised to the patient, who said cheerfully, 'Not to worry, Nurse. I'm sure you didn't do it on purpose.'

Together Liz and Justin bent over the bed, their heads close as they examined the wound. Paula would have liked to leave them and slip away but she knew she would be required to apply a fresh dressing and so she remained in the background. Fixing her eyes on a procession of white woolly clouds beyond the window, she schooled herself to accept the situation.

There would be countless incidents like this in the future. If she let herself be torn apart over every single one of them, she would become a nervous wreck. Resolutely she forced herself to present an appearance of cool detachment.

Yet even that was wrong.

Her mind actually had wandered a little when she suddenly realised Liz was addressing her.

'Are you still with us, Nurse? Then perhaps you'd be good enough to re-dress the wound.'

Flushed with annoyance, Paula pressed herself against the curtain to allow the two doctors to pass. She hadn't meant to look at Justin but somehow she didn't seem able to help herself. For one brief second their eyes met but the expression in his was so surprising that she was left feeling utterly bewildered.

He couldn't possibly have looked *sad* . . . Maybe it was embarrassment because she had practically asked for a rebuke. Well, it wouldn't happen again. In future she would make quite sure she kept her mind on the job.

For a while she managed to avoid Liz altogether but Justin frequently visited the ward by himself. One evening when Paula was about to go off duty, he came in quietly to see an operation patient who was requiring special treatment.

Paula should have left the ward ten minutes earlier but she had paused to talk to an eighteen-year-old boy who was to have his appendix removed the following day. He was in a highly nervous state and full of questions.

'How long shall I be unconscious? Are you sure I shan't feel anything?' He glanced across the ward to where Justin and a staff nurse stood by the other patient's bed. 'Is that the bloke who'll do it?'

'I don't know but it's very likely,' Paula said. 'He does a lot of operations.'

'He's good, is he?' Peter asked eagerly.

'Oh yes, very good indeed.'

'I wish you'd ask him. I'd like to know for sure he's the one. I wouldn't want it to be that other guy. He doesn't look much older than me.'

'I expect you mean Dr Carlton. He's at least seven years older than you are and quite capable of taking your appendix out. It's really a very simple operation, you know.' Paula smiled as she spoke, understanding that to the patient even the most routine operation was of enormous importance.

'I still wouldn't want him to mess about with me.' Peter clutched at her arm. 'Looks like that older doctor is just leaving, Nurse. Can't you stop him?'

'Let me go and I'll have a word with him.'

Resigned to the necessity of approaching Justin, she waylaid him as he passed with Staff Nurse Janet Coates, who was in her thirties and Sister's main support.

'Excuse me, Doctor. Could you spare a minute to talk to Peter? He's very worried about tomorrow.'

'He's been ordered sedatives,' the staff nurse told her.

'Yes, I know, but I think he needs a few words of reassurance.'

'Of course I'll come,' Justin said. 'Did you want me for anything else, Staff?'

'No, thank you.' She passed a hand wearily over her forehead.

'Have you got a headache?' he asked. 'If so, go and dose yourself with something before you go off duty.'

'It's been aching all day. I think I'll have an early night.'

He looked after her as she walked away, seemed about to say something to Paula and then changed his mind.

'Aren't you making yourself late?' he asked. 'It's nearly fifteen minutes past eight.'

'I couldn't leave Peter to lie there worrying all by himself and the night nurses are all busy.'

She had spoken very quietly but now she dropped her voice even lower. 'He wants to know if you're doing the operation. He seems to think you're trustworthy.'

Justin smiled. 'I'll try and convince him he's got nothing to bother about.'

'But are you?' Paula persisted.

'Er—no. I think it's going to be Liz.'

'Oh dear—he won't like that,' she exclaimed in dismay.

It was impossible for her to remain and listen to the conversation, and she went to the locker room to remove her apron before leaving. The last thing she wanted was to emerge as Justin came past on his way out and she lingered to talk to two other day nurses who were still there.

Having given him a good five minutes with Peter, she opened the door and looked out, only to find him just coming through the swing doors. It was exactly as though she had planned her own departure to coincide with his.

There was nothing for it but to put a good face on it and ask if he had been successful.

'Yes, I think so,' Justin said. 'He wouldn't have Liz at any price so I took the easy way out and promised to do it myself.'

Agreeably surprised, and for a moment actually forgetting all that lay between them, Paula spoke

easily and naturally. 'I do think that was nice of
you, but what will the RSO say about the switch?'

'He's a reasonable sort of chap. I don't think he'll
mind.'

They walked on together, out into the open air
and across the garden until their routes divided.
The moment of friendly communication had been
short-lived and when Justin asked how she was
liking Bradshaw his voice was stiff and he stared
straight ahead.

'I'm getting used to it. I wasn't sure about Sister
at first but she's not so bad. I like the patients, of
course, and it's marvellous to have them all conscious and capable of conversation.'

'Did you enjoy your holiday?' he asked.

'What holiday?' Paula turned to him in astonishment and then hastily looked away.

'You disappeared for two weeks. I assumed you
were on holiday.'

'I was at West City, working very hard at block
study. I had most of my holiday in the spring.'

'I should think you could do with another after
spending all the summer at St Andrews,' Justin
said. He changed the subject abruptly. 'By the way,
I felt a bit concerned about that staff nurse. To my
mind she looked really ill.'

'A bad headache can make anybody look awful.
She'll probably be okay in the morning.'

But Paula was wrong. Staff Nurse Coates did not
turn up for duty at seven-forty-five, and when Sister

gathered the nurses together for the daily report she told them that she had been taken to the sick bay with a high temperature.

'It's really very awkward,' she fussed. 'Staff Nurse was such a dependable person and we're short enough as it is, due to people being away on holiday. I've told Miss Wallace that I really must have someone to take her place even if she's only off for a few days.'

'Do you know what's the matter with her, Sister?' Jenny asked.

'No, of course I don't. I don't suppose anyone does at present.'

By the following day everyone in the ward—except the patients, from whom the information was carefully withheld—knew that the staff nurse was suffering from a bad attack of summer flu.

'They're sending us a temporary replacement from West City,' Sister said. She picked up a piece of paper. 'Staff Nurse Shipton. I'm sure you'll all do your best to cooperate with her.'

CHAPTER TEN

PAULA's gasp of dismay was quickly stifled. They needed somebody of Mary's quality to replace Staff Nurse Coates and it was absurd to let herself wish— even for a moment—that some other nurse had been chosen.

Mary would not be arriving until the afternoon, Sister told them, and they would just have to manage as best they could during the morning.

'It would have to be an operation day,' Jenny grumbled as she whisked past Paula carrying someone's pre-med tablets on a saucer. 'Oh, heavens, here's a doctor descending on us! What on earth does she want so early in the morning?'

Liz advanced with a purposeful air. 'I've come to check on my operation patients,' she announced. 'We're not starting on the list for another half-hour.'

'None of them is giving any cause for concern,' Sister told her shortly. Her eye alighted on Paula. 'Go with Dr Deben, Nurse, and give her any information she requires.'

Paula accepted the task reluctantly but there were no problems until they reached Peter's bed. Having been well sedated, he was half asleep but he looked up in surprise as they halted beside him.

Sensing that he was about to ask what on earth Liz wanted, Paula spoke hastily in an under-tone.

'This one has been transferred to Dr Stewart's list. Didn't he tell you?'

'I haven't seen him since yesterday lunchtime. Are you sure you haven't made a mistake?'

'Quite sure. I was here when the alteration was made.'

'Well, I know nothing about it.' Liz stared at the patient, frowning and then—to Paula's relief—moved farther away. 'What *is* all this nonsense, Nurse? Does Peter imagine I'm incapable of taking out a simple appendix, or is there some other reason?'

'Oh—er—I think he's got an objection to women doctors. He's a very nervous type of boy and—'

'I'm perfectly aware that he's nervous but it doesn't do to give in to phobias of that sort. Who authorised the change? Was it the RSO?'

'N-no, it was Dr Stewart himself.'

'Well, really!' Liz was obviously outraged. 'I never heard of such a thing. Justin has absolutely no right to mess about with my list.'

'I'm sure he will be able to explain it all to you when he gets a chance—'

'There had better be a good explanation,' Liz said grimly. 'I'm very much obliged to you, Nurse, for putting me in the picture.'

She went striding off and Paula resumed her

interrupted work. It was impossible not to feel a faint feeling of satisfaction because there was going to be trouble between Justin and Liz; she wouldn't have been human if she hadn't felt like that. But it never occurred to her that she might actually witness it.

All the morning the Bradshaw nurses—in addition to their normal duties—were escorting patients to the theatre and fetching them back. To Peter's delight he was allotted to Paula's charge and they set off about mid-morning.

Some of his nervousness had returned, in spite of the sedation, and he clung without embarrassment to her hand as they went down the corridor. The theatre porter, who had summed up the situation at a glance, made no comment and nurse and patient arrived at the anaesthetics room still linked.

'You'll stay with me until I go under,' Peter begged.

'Yes, of course,' Paula promised. 'I don't suppose you'll have to wait long.'

At West City the surgeons frequently worked on for hours without a break but at St Andrews there was time for coffee. Unfortunately Paula's arrival with the trolley had coincided with a ten-minute interval which the RSO had permitted.

Justin and Liz were both in the anaesthetics room. All her bright hair was hidden beneath the ugly theatre cap but she had pulled off her mask and still contrived to look attractive. His expression was sombre and it was immediately clear to Paula that they were in the middle of a row.

'This is the one,' Liz snapped as she saw Peter's anxious face.

She spoke very quietly and it was only because Paula was so alert to the situation between them that she was able to make out what was being said. Peter, facing the other way, appeared unaware of what was going on.

'I've been waiting all the morning to have this out with you,' Liz went on. 'I very much resent your interfering with my patients behind my back.'

Justin's grey eyes were bright with sudden anger. 'It was pure chance that it happened behind your back, as you call it. If you'd been available yesterday I would have told you about it at once.'

'*Told me* indeed! Hasn't it occurred to you that I might have been consulted before the change was made?'

With an obvious effort he got a grip on his temper. 'It just wasn't practicable, love. That boy was working himself up into a serious state of panic. Something had to be done to reassure him.' He put his hand on her shoulder and gently turned her to face him. 'Do be reasonable, Liz. It's not like you to make such a fuss.'

'I'm sorry.' Her brilliant smile flashed out. 'I guess I'm a bit on edge myself these days. Forgive me?'

'Of course.' His answering smile pierced Paula's

heart like a knife. 'Drink up your coffee and let's get on.'

Luckily the anaesthetist appeared just then and took charge of the patient. Paula waited until the hand she was holding relaxed and then returned to the ward. There was so much to do that it was impossible for her to dwell on the incident, and when the summons came to go and fetch Peter back to the ward she did not see either Justin or Liz.

Mary arrived immediately after lunch. She came in with Sister and was introduced to one or two nurses, including Paula.

Very smart in her blue dress and red belt, she looked extremely sure of herself and not at all like the new girl among people who were all used to working together.

'Nurse Garland and I know each other quite well,' she told Sister.

'Really? Then she can show you round and tell you about the patients.'

Most of them were resting and the two girls walked round quietly. As Paula answered questions she could sense Mary's agile brain storing it all up like a computer. No doubt, before long, she would know as much about the ward as Sister.

'How about yourself, Paula?' Mary asked as they finished their tour. 'How are you making out at St Andrews?'

'Okay, I hope, but this is only my second ward. I've got a year to do here.'

'I expect you'll pass the exam the second time if you make up your mind to it,' Mary said kindly. 'It's strange you and I should meet up like this. I don't suppose we've got rooms next to each other? That really would be a coincidence.'

'I've no idea where your room is,' Paula said shortly. 'It's not likely to be next to me because I'm at the end of the lower corridor and the nurse next door is still in possession, as far as I know.'

She would have been glad to learn that Mary had been accommodated upstairs, but later that day she discovered that she was quite close after all, on the other side of the passage. Not that it mattered very much. Janet Coates would soon be back and then Mary would return to West City.

But unfortunately Janet's bout of flu turned out to be very severe and she was kept in the sick bay for two weeks, after which she went home to convalesce.

'I shall be thankful when she comes back,' Jenny sighed one day. 'That Mary Shipton is too perfect for me. Was she always like this?'

'Always,' Paula asserted solemnly. 'She has never in her whole life done anything wrong.'

Both girls laughed but with a undercurrent of bitterness. In Jenny's case it was probably quite unimportant, but Paula was unhappily aware that for her a great deal of the joy had gone out of nursing. She had actually been accused that morning of not knowing how to make a bed properly and she had had to set her lips with real determination in order not to make a sharp reply which would have put her in the wrong.

What with trying to please Mary, and the daily torture of seeing Justin and Liz, she was becoming more and more depressed. Some sort of antidote was obviously necessary and she suddenly thought of Kevin.

She hadn't seen him for quite a while and it was surprising that he hadn't rung up to complain. She resolved to walk to Parkside Avenue and visit No 24 on her next free afternoon.

Just to be on the safe side, she rang up the evening before. Mrs Blake answered the phone.

'We were only saying the other day we hadn't heard anything of you lately, dear.' She sounded delighted. 'Yes, of course come round tomorrow. Kevin is ever so much better and he'll be thrilled to see you. He's out just now or I'd get him to the phone.'

'Out?' Paula asked in surprise. 'Is he fit enough to be out and about as late as this?'

'Well, we didn't think it would hurt him. He's with some friends who've taken him for a drive. I didn't try to dissuade him because I was so glad he was willing to go out in a car after what happened. See you tomorrow then, dear.'

'It's Saturday,' Paula said doubtfully. 'Since he's suddenly become so mobile perhaps he'll want to go out again.'

'He certainly won't if he knows he's going to see you. Come round as soon as you can get away and we'll be looking out for you.'

It was three o'clock before she was ready to start. She had been late leaving the ward and so tired that she was obliged to sit down in her room before she summoned enough energy to change. Luckily she wasn't on duty again until Sunday morning so she would be able to stay at Kevin's house throughout the evening as well if he invited her.

Since there wasn't much left of the afternoon, she hoped very much that he would.

There was a slight suggestion of autumn in the air although the sun was hot. In the shade it was definitely chilly and the fresh air was very invigorating. Paula quickened her pace and allowed herself, just for a moment, to think how lovely it would be at Seagate.

She came to Kevin's house and dismissed all thoughts of Seagate from her mind. As she waited for the door bell to be answered she heard sounds of young voices coming from the direction of the garden. Or was it perhaps from next door? That seemed much more likely, she decided, and was consequently astonished to find the door flung open by a girl with long light brown hair who looked about eighteen.

'Hullo!' She smiled uncertainly and waited for Paula to say what she wanted.

'I came to see Kevin—that is, I wondered how he was. Is he in?'

'Oh yes—he's in the garden. Are you Paula, the girl who used to nurse him? He said something about you coming round this afternoon.' She opened the door wider with an hospitable air. 'Come right in.'

Paula stepped over the familiar threshold with a strong feeling of unreality. The voices were much louder now and there was a sound of someone strumming a guitar.

'Are you having a party?' she asked.

'Not a party. Kevin's not really up to that yet.' She led the way down the hall, talking over her shoulder. 'My name's Vicky, by the way. I expect Kevin will introduce you to the others.'

There was no sign of Mr and Mrs Blake. Vicky took her through the empty lounge and out by the french windows. There was a small group of two young men and another girl sitting in comfortable chairs on the lawn.

Kevin looked round and, seeing Paula, got quickly to his feet. For a moment she forgot the others as she stared at him, noting with immense pleasure the improvement in his appearance; cheeks lightly tanned and no longer hollow, eyes bright and without the haunted look and black shadows.

'It's great to see you!' he exclaimed. He came forward to meet her and kissed her lightly. 'You look absolutely worn out. Come and sit down and we'll all wait on you.'

'I'm not as bad as that,' Paula protested, laughing. 'I just need to put my feet up for a bit.'

A boy with very fair hair got up and gave her his chair, insisting on sitting on the grass. The second girl sat silently on the other side of Kevin, their hands touching between their chairs. Looking round at them Paula thought what a nice bunch they seemed—and how very, very young.

Suddenly it seemed to her that they belonged to a different generation from herself, although they were all close in age. Even Kevin, in spite of his shattering experience, hadn't been aged by it. Rather the opposite, in fact.

They were very nice to her and waited on her at tea-time, treating her—she thought with wry amusement—rather like an invalid aunt. But in spite of their attentions she felt herself very much the odd one out. She resolutely refused an invitation to stay on after tea and left about half-past five.

Kevin came to the front door with her.

'I'm so glad you're beginning to pick up the threads again,' she said warmly. 'Do you know when you'll be allowed to go back to work?'

'Not for another month.' He took her hand, intertwining his fingers with hers. 'I'll be glad when the time comes. I'm getting restless now.'

'I can understand that.'

'You understand pretty well everything about your patients, don't you, Paula? I'll never forget how much you've helped me.'

'I did hardly anything,' she said unsteadily. 'And if you only knew it, you've been quite a help to me.'

He looked at her in astonishment. 'I don't see how.'

'You can take my word for it it's true.' She had no intention of explaining. 'Goodbye, Kevin. Take care of yourself.'

'My Mum will see to that. Be seeing you, Paula. Don't forget to keep in touch.'

She smiled and let him take that as agreement if he wanted to. But as she walked down the road she felt quite sure that they were unlikely to meet again, except perhaps by accident. It was better that way; he obviously no longer needed her help. As for herself, she had got to soldier on and somehow conquer the way she felt about Justin before it got her down completely.

Her spell of working in Bradshaw wouldn't go on for ever and after that the authorities would surely move her to a medical ward. She wouldn't see nearly as much of Justin then and it would be easier to persevere with her determination to remove him completely from her mind and heart.

On the Monday after her visit to Kevin something happened which made her all the more determined.

'Guess what!' Jenny came into the locker room obviously bursting with an interesting item of news.

'You're apparently going to tell us so why should we bother with guessing?' asked another second year nurse. 'Get on with it or we'll all be late on duty.'

Curiosity made Paula pause with her hand on the door knob. Therefore she had her back turned when Jenny dropped her bombshell.

She was to be very grateful for that.

'My boy friend took me to the King's Arms for a drink last evening and while we were there Justin and Liz came in. They didn't see us but actually we were quite close to them when they sat down at a small table in a corner.'

'What's so interesting about that?' someone asked.

'Give me a chance. I have to explain how it all happened.'

'She's only trying to make it more dramatic. I don't suppose it's anything much really.'

'Yes it is then!' Jenny took a deep breath. 'Liz was wearing an engagement ring—an absolutely super emerald. I saw it quite plainly because she had her hand on the table—so as to show it off, I expect, and I don't blame her either. It must have cost a packet.'

'Everybody knew those two were going to get fixed up one day,' a third-year nurse said in a superior tone. 'You can't pretend it's surprising.'

There was a sudden rush for the door. They all surged past Paula leaving her standing there blindly.

Like the others she had known it was going to happen. But she would never have believed it would hurt so much.

CHAPTER ELEVEN

'I'M fed up!' Tony announced. He looked tired, with tiny lines at the corners of his eyes Paula couldn't remember noticing before.

'That makes two of us.'

She had spoken lightly and even managed a smile but he detected the depression which she struggled to hide.

'What's up with you then?' he asked. 'Sister been upsetting you?'

'Oh no. She's okay when you get used to her. I guess I just need a holiday. It seems a very long time since the one I had earlier in the year.'

'Me too.' He yawned prodigiously. 'I've been on duty for thirty-six hours non-stop and I'm dead on my feet.'

Paula looked at him sympathetically. Even at a small place like St Andrews housemen sometimes had to work very long hours but it was unusual for Tony to complain. He usually contrived to remain cheerful under all circumstances.

'Are you free this evening?' she asked. 'Better get an early night.'

They were talking in the ward kitchen where Tony had gone to beg a cup of tea. It was just before the evening rush and Paula had a few minutes to spare.

'I'm released from the treadmill the same time as you,' he said. 'In other words—eight o'clock. But I don't really fancy just going off to bed, however sensible your advice may be. I'd much rather go out and get drunk. How about you coming with me?'

'Not to get drunk,' she told him firmly. 'It's not my idea of fun, thank you. But I'd be glad to go with you to a pub and have *one* drink.'

'I won't take you unless you promise to be rash and have a couple.'

'I might even do that,' she conceded.

They met in the lounge of the Nurses' Home and walked slowly down the road hand-in-hand. The touch of his fingers was comforting and in her secret heart Paula acknowledged that she was becoming very fond of Tony. Not that the gentle warmth she felt towards him bore any resemblance to the white-hot flame of her love for Justin, but his company was pleasant and—on the whole—undemanding.

Both were cheered by the conviviality they found in the pub, and their very modest consumption of alcohol, but they did not stay long for he was having difficulty in keeping his eyes open.

'There was something I wanted to ask you,' he said as they returned at an even slower pace to the hospital. 'But my brain is completely addled and I can't think what it is.'

'I expect you'll remember some time.'

Paula spoke absently, not paying much attention, but a moment later she was jolted out of her abstraction by a sudden exclamation.

'Dead on cue!' He held out his hand with a button in it. 'This has been loose for days and I kept meaning to ask you to sew it on for me. I was fiddling with it just now, I suppose, and it came right off.'

'Of course I'll sew it on.' Paula glanced at her watch by the light of a street lamp. 'It's only about ten-fifteen so I might as well do it tonight.'

'Is it as early as that?' he asked in surprise. 'Okay then—I'll come back to the Nurses' Home with you.'

She had taken it for granted that he would wait in the lounge while she fetched her sewing materials, but when she reached her room she found him behind her.

It was against the rules but somehow it didn't seem to matter. The job would only take a few minutes and then Tony would go away again. The risk of discovery was really very slight.

She threaded her needle and sat down in the chair. There was nowhere except the bed for Tony and he stretched out on it comfortably.

'Nice little domestic scene,' he said with a grin.

'If you really want to know,' Paula told him, 'I *hate* sewing on buttons and I wouldn't do it for anybody but you, Tony love.'

He smiled at her lazily and his eyelids drooped. As Paula stitched on she thought a little bitterly how easily and naturally that sort of lie slipped off the tongue. She would sew twenty buttons on for Justin and do it willingly—if he ever asked her.

It was difficult to imagine Liz engaged in such a mundane task.

Tony was asleep. The deepening of his breathing told her that and she knew she ought to wake him. But it was only ten forty-five; he could have another ten minutes anyway.

Paula put her needle and cotton away and leaned back in the chair, allowing her thoughts to wander. Sweet and idle dreams were all she had to sustain her these days and her starving heart found them poor nourishment. Nevertheless she allowed herself to drift wistfully on a tide of might-have-been until an exclamation from Tony jerked her back to the present.

'God—it's eleven-thirty!' He was sitting up and looking at his watch. 'Why didn't you wake me?'

Paula glanced at her own. 'It can't be as late as that—at least I don't think so. I only make it just on eleven, but you'll have to hurry.'

'Afraid you're wrong, Paula. I checked mine at six o'clock and it was okay then. But not to worry, I'll exit by the window like I did before.' He swung his feet to the floor.

'Hang on for a few minutes. I'll make sure first that my watch really is slow—'

'Don't be daft,' he interrupted. 'The Warden's probably locking up right now and you don't want her to suspect you've got a bloke in your room.'

'I don't see why she should think that.'

'Nasty suspicious minds, Wardens generally have. Take my advice and keep your door shut. I'll nip out as soon as I've pulled myself together.'

Desperately worried, Paula stood silently waiting for him to go. Tony yawned and stretched, rubbing his eyes, and then moved over to the window.

'I'll be off now,' he announced cheerfully. 'Thanks a lot for the sewing.'

'Just a minute!' She moved hastily to the light switch. 'I'd better put the light out before you draw the curtains back.'

Plunged into darkness, she heard the curtain rattle. And then another sound froze the blood in her veins so that she stood incapable of movement or of speech, conscious only of total panic.

Someone was knocking on the door.

'Don't open it!' Tony hissed. 'Let me get out first.'

But the person at the door didn't wait for an invitation to enter. It hadn't occurred to Paula to lock it and it opened slowly and cautiously, letting in a stream of light from the corridor.

'I'm sorry to barge in like this, Paula,' Mary Shipton said coldly, 'but I felt sure I could hear a man's voice in here. I suppose you know it's past eleven? And in any case you aren't supposed to have male visitors in your room?'

At the window Tony swung round and faced her. 'What the hell has it got to do with you?'

'I happen to be a senior nurse and it's obviously my duty to see the rules are kept.' She glanced round disapprovingly and Paula felt sure she had noted the rumpled bed. 'Don't you think it would be a good idea to put the light on?'

'No, I don't!' he snapped as Paula still seemed incapable of speech. 'I prefer to make my escape in the dark for obvious reasons.'

It didn't seem to have occurred to him that there was now no need for secrecy, Paula reflected unhappily. Or was he perhaps right to be careful? Maybe Mary didn't intend to do any more than throw her weight about as a staff nurse?

She was soon undeceived.

'I'm really sorry about this,' Mary said when they were alone, 'but I don't see I've any option but to tell the Warden and Miss Wallace what's been going on.'

'Nothing's been going on!' Paula flashed. 'If you really want to know, I was sewing a button on for Tony and he fell asleep. My watch was slow and I didn't know it was locking up time.'

'Oh dear!' Mary looked down her nose in a superior sort of way. 'I'm afraid that sounds a dreadfully phoney story. Besides, Tony shouldn't have been in here at all.'

'He followed me when I went to fetch my needle and cotton.'

'But you didn't have to let him remain.'

Paula shrugged. 'We were only going to be here a few minutes. I've just told you he fell asleep.'

Mary hesitated and then said earnestly, 'I really do hate the thought of reporting you and, of course, I believe every word you've said, even though it does sound terribly improbable. And yet it's obviously my duty to tell on you. If nurses think they can get away with this sort of thing, goodness knows where it may lead.'

'It's not going to lead me anywhere—I can tell you that for a start.'

'But it's the principle of the thing—'

Suddenly Paula could bear it no longer. If Mary thought she was going to get down on her knees and beg for mercy, then she'd got another think coming. Her own conscience was perfectly clear. If the Warden and Miss Wallace and everybody else didn't choose to believe her story, then that was just too bad.

'Okay, so it's the principle—' She clenched her fists as she clung to the last shreds of her temper. 'I'm sure that must be a great satisfaction to you, because you mean to report me, don't you? And I don't care anyway! Go ahead and do it, that's all I've got to say.' She flung open the door which Mary had closed behind her. 'And now, for heaven's sake, get out of my room.'

Mary left with a look of deep reproach and Paula knew she'd burnt her boats. If she had pleaded there might have been just a chance, but it was gone now. She'd thrown it away deliberately and she would have to take what was certainly coming to her as best she could.

Somehow it didn't seem to matter as much as it should have done, though she suspected that there might be bitter regrets in the near future.

Both bitterness and regret descended on her in full measure during the sleepless hours of the night. Was it all to be wasted, the long uphill struggle she'd had ever since she failed her exam? She'd tried so hard at St Andrews and she'd been successful too, in many ways. Anne Knox had given her a good report and she was doing all right in Bradshaw, on the whole.

She would get on better still when Mary had returned to West City. If she was to be allowed to remain.

She was not kept long in suspense. Miss Wallace sent for her the following afternoon. This time she wasn't told to 'come along when she was off duty.' It was a definite summons.

'Well, Nurse Garland?' The Nursing Officer was looking very grave. 'Once more you are in trouble and this time it seems to be extremely serious. Is it true that Dr Carlton was in your room at the Nurses' Home last night after locking up time?'

'Yes, Miss Wallace.' Paula tilted her head and met the accusing eyes with coolness and determination although her heart was thudding with nervous tension. 'Please may I tell you exactly what happened?'

'I am most anxious to know.'

She took a deep breath and plunged in, telling her story as carefully and clearly as if she had been in the witness box. Miss Wallace listened without interruption but Paula noted with a sinking heart that her expression had not altered.

'This really is a most extraordinary account, Nurse. I'm prepared to accept that the incident may have started innocently with the button being sewn on, though you know perfectly well you were breaking a very strict rule. But to say that your watch was slow really does seem to me to be a very feeble excuse and one which I regard as distinctly suspect.'

'It's true, Miss Wallace,' Paula insisted. 'I wouldn't have made it up because—well, it *does* sound so weak. And Dr Carlton had dropped off— he'd been on duty for a day and a half and was exhausted—so I thought I'd leave him undisturbed until the last possible moment.'

'It would have been far more sensible to send him off to his own bed,' Miss Wallace said severely.

Had she accepted the story after all? Hope leapt to life in Paula but received no encouragement from the Nursing Officer's general demeanour. She sat waiting with downcast eyes, her hands tightly twisted together in her lap.

'You realise that this is the second time I've had to have a serious talk with you?' Miss Wallace continued after a pause for thought. 'And both times there was a man involved. This is a grave reflection on your character, Nurse.'

It wasn't fair . . . Rebellious thoughts flooded Paula's mind. She might have been a bit like that in the past, but not now. Definitely not now.

'However, I've decided to accept your story as being mostly true, though that doesn't mean I'm condoning your behaviour. You will have to be punished and I shall tell the Warden that you are not to be given any late passes for a month. I also want you to realise that I shan't be so lenient if there is any more of this sort of thing. This is your very last chance, Nurse Garland.'

'Thank you, Miss Wallace.' Eager to escape, Paula stood up and, receiving a gesture of dismissal, fled from the room.

The late passes didn't matter. She had scarcely had any since coming to St Andrews. But the warning was a different thing altogether. She would have to be painfully careful in future if she wanted to remain at St Andrews and take the exam again.

Did she *really* want to stay? Walking across the garden on her way back to the ward Paula faced the prospect honestly and knew herself doubtful.

Before long Liz and Justin would get married, but presumably they would still be working here. How could she ever hope to cure herself of this hopeless love under such circumstances?

The relentless questions hammered at her brain and she could not find the answers. She was in the sort of mood when the smallest thing could tip the balance, and such an incident occurred the same afternoon.

Among the patients under her special care was a man with high blood pressure. He had had an operation two days ago but it was still necessary to check his condition every half-hour. Paula had done this before she went to see Miss Wallace and had expected to be back in plenty of time for the next recording.

Unfortunately she had so much on her mind that it slipped her memory until ten minutes past the proper time.

There was no harm done and no one would ever have known anything about it if Sister had not been on duty that afternoon. When Paula hurried to the bedside she found that the chart had already been filled in.

'I see you have remembered, Nurse,' said an acid voice as she replaced the chart and turned away. 'What's your excuse this time? Your watch slow again?'

Paula flushed with mingled embarrassment and annoyance. Obviously Sister Leyton knew all about the trouble she was in and all the details too. She would be very much on the look out in future.

She said rapidly, 'I'm sorry, Sister,' and made no attempt to explain her loss of memory. It would have been a waste of time anyway.

Tomorrow was her day off and she felt she needed it. She resolved to go off by herself to some place where she could be quite alone, and to spend the day thinking very seriously about her future.

It seemed more than probable that she would return to St Andrews determined to give in her notice.

Where should she go? Somewhere by bus seemed the best suggestion and she set out after breakfast to walk to the bus station, determined to get on the first one which had a suitable destination.

She was staring at the red monsters lined up before her when the painfully familiar roar of a sports car caught her ear. Instinctively turning to look, she saw Justin drawing up outside a nearby paper shop. It was Sunday, she remembered; maybe he'd got a free day too.

In a panic in case he should see her, she leapt on the nearest bus and sat down on the far side. It was already nearly full and the driver climbed up into his seat shortly afterwards.

'Where to?' the conductor asked, appearing at her side.

'Oh—er—I'm not sure.' Paula struggled not to

give an impression of lunacy. 'How far are you going?'

'Seagate's our terminus, miss, but you don't have to go all the way if you don't want to.' He rattled off a list of intermediate stops. 'Take your pick.'

Seagate . . . It promised nothing but painful memories and yet was extraordinarily tempting. And it would certainly be a good place for quiet thought.

'I'll travel all the way, please,' Paula said, adding as an afterthought, 'A return ticket. What time shall I be able to get back?'

There were only two return buses and she thought she would take the later one, since her decision was going to be a very difficult one to make.

It seemed a long, long way—much farther than when she had travelled in Justin's sports car. But at last they reached the marshes, stretching flat and empty on either side of the road, and then the wide main street of Seagate. Stiff after sitting for so long, Paula got out near the hotel and looked about her, wondering where to make for.

As she hesitated, a snatch of conversation between the driver and conductor penetrated her consciousness.

'That chap's still there. Followed us all the way from Belton Park.'

'Must have driven him dotty, keeping behind a bus in a car like that. It takes all sorts—!'

Automatically Paula followed the direction of their amused gaze. And she saw that the mysterious follower of the bus was Justin.

CHAPTER TWELVE

JUSTIN leapt out and came striding towards her. He seized her by the arm and started to propel her towards his car.

'Come on, Paula—we can't talk here.'

'I don't want to talk.' Furious at his high-handed treatment, she began to struggle fiercely. 'Let me go at once! We've got nothing to say to each other.'

'On the contrary, we've got a very great deal. Or, at least, *I*'ve got a lot to say to you and I intend to say it whether you like it or not.'

Aware that the driver and conductor of the bus were still watching with interest, Paula submitted. She got into the car and sat rigidly upright, desperately trying to still the thudding of her heart.

'You've got a nerve, kidnapping me like this,' she snapped as soon as she could control her voice. 'Why on earth did you do it?'

'It was a sudden impulse, when I saw you get on the Seagate bus.' He reversed into a gateway. 'I thought maybe we could talk here, in these lovely peaceful surroundings, and I wouldn't make such a mess of it as I've done in the past.'

'I don't see that it can possibly make the slightest difference. You can't alter facts.' As the car shot down the road she stole a glance at his grim, set face. 'Like me to do a bit of re-capping for you?'

'There's no need. I haven't forgotten one single thing about you and me.' He braked at a corner and turned towards the river bank.

Not *that* way, Paula almost cried aloud. And at the same moment, as though to emphasise the difference between last time and this, it began to rain.

'Oh, hell!' Justin glanced angrily up at the sky. 'I suppose I'd better stop and put the hood up.'

'Please yourself.'

'If that's how you feel about it, I won't bother just yet. Perhaps it's only a light shower.'

At first the windscreen deflected the rain over their heads. But as they drew near the sailing club it began to drive in at the sides.

'It's no good,' Justin said. 'We'll have to stop or we'll both get soaked.' The little car skidded slightly on the wet road as he halted abruptly. 'Afraid we'll have to talk in the car, Paula.'

'There isn't going to be any talk—that is, not in the sense you mean. How many more times have I got to tell you?'

Ignoring her comment he jumped out and began to struggle with the hood. Paula stared straight ahead, desperately trying to give an appearance of total detachment.

But it was no good. Justin was obviously having problems and after a while she joined him in the narrow muddy road and stiffly offered her help.

Neither of them noticed the car coming towards them at some speed, and the driver at first did not seem to realise that there were two people wrestling with a hood which had stuck halfway.

Justin was the first to become aware of their danger. To her amazement, Paula felt a violent push which sent her sprawling onto the grass, where she landed with her face in the wet undergrowth.

Gasping but unhurt, she scrambled to her feet and looked to see why she had received such extraordinary treatment. She even started to call out, 'What do you think you're doing?' and then broke off in horror.

Justin was lying in the road behind his car. He was very still, his face hidden in his outstretched arms and the rain pouring down on his unprotected body. A few yards farther on there was a stationary car and a middle-aged man in sailing gear was jumping out.

'I swear I never saw him!' He came running down the road. 'My God—is he dead?'

An icy sick terror held Paula by the throat but somehow she managed to pull herself together. 'No, of course not. Can't you see he's started to move?'

As she went down on her knees, Justin turned very slowly onto his back and looked at her blankly.

There was mud on his forehead and she dabbed at it gently with her handkerchief.

'I only hit him a glancing blow—I didn't run over him,' the man insisted. 'Perhaps he banged his head against his own car.'

'I'm okay.' Justin glanced at him as he began to struggle to his feet. 'I reckon it was as much my fault as yours. I didn't notice you coming until it was too late to get out of the way.'

But there had been time enough to ensure *her* safety, Paula thought gratefully.

'Take it easy,' she begged. 'You may be more hurt than you realise.'

'Perhaps he ought to see a doctor?' suggested the owner of the other car.

'I *am* a doctor.' Justin smiled faintly. 'So there's no need for you to worry any more.'

'Well, if you're sure you're all right, old chap, I'll be on my way.' The man seemed greatly relieved and a moment later he drove off towards the club-house.

Neither of them noticed his departure. Justin was leaning against his car, his face very white and lines of pain round his mouth, and Paula watched him anxiously.

'There *is* something wrong, isn't there?' she said quietly. 'Please tell me what it is.'

'My shoulder. I landed on it with considerable force.'

'It's not dislocated?'

'No. But I'm afraid the collar bone is broken.' He interrupted her exclamation of distress. 'Are you all right?'

'Yes, of course, but it was all due to you. If you hadn't pushed me I'd probably have been hit as well.'

'I can't take any credit for it. It was instinctive reaction.'

Paula lowered her eyes hastily and began to grope in the pocket of her anorak. 'It's such a shame you've got hurt. Why on earth did you let that man think you were unharmed?' She produced a scarf and began to fold it.

'It seemed simpler that way.' He was watching her busy fingers. 'Are you going to strap me up?'

'That was the idea.' She steeled herself to work coolly and calmly when all the time she longed to fling her arms round him and tell him how sorry she was.

Carefully and tenderly she strapped his arm against his body, so that he was spared the agony of movement. The rain streamed down on them, plastering their hair against their foreheads and running into their eyes but neither of them noticed the discomfort. Paula was intent only on her work but Justin's face wore a strange expression.

'There!' She finished tying the knot. 'Does that feel better?'

'Much. You've made a very good job of it.'

He had spoken in such a curiously abstracted

tone that she looked at him in surprise. 'What's the matter?'

'There's something you don't seem to have thought of.'

'What?' She gazed at him, her eyes dilating in nameless fear.

So far she had thought only of his injury and what she could do to ease it. But now—suddenly and with tremendous force—the full implication of it hit her.

'Oh God—' She put both hands over her face. 'You won't be able to drive.'

'Afraid not, love. It's my left shoulder and I have to change gear on that side. If it had been the right—'

'It still wouldn't have been safe. Oh, Justin—whatever are we going to do? You ought to get to hospital as quickly as possible.'

There was a pause which was so charged with meaning that it could almost be felt. Paula's hands dropped to her sides in a gesture of despair as Justin made no reply.

She said frantically, 'You want me to drive, don't you? But I can't—you know I never drive now. It's—it's impossible—'

'You've still got your licence?'

'Oh yes, but—' She stared at him appealingly. 'You don't know what you're asking.'

Justin again did not speak but he put his right arm round her and held her close to him. She was shaking all over, partly because of what had just happened but mostly because she knew—quite clearly and irrevocably—that she would have to conquer her fear. For his sake.

Suddenly she lifted her head. 'All right—I'll do it. But you'll have to be very patient with me.'

'I knew you'd rise to the occasion.' Justin smiled and kissed her wet face.

His lips were cold and it was strange that their touch should kindle such a flame in Paula. She stood trembling within the circle of his arm, longing only to pour out her love for him.

But there was too much between them, and among all the doubts and misunderstandings of the past his engagement to Liz stood out like a great rock. Nothing could ever explain *that* away.

'I think you'd better give me some driving instruction,' she said in a small voice.

He gave her a quick hug and released her. 'Get in the car and I'll show you where everything is. You'll soon feel at home.'

Doubting that very much, Paula obeyed. It seemed strange to sit in the driver's seat with Justin on her left. But fortunately the car itself presented no difficulties though her lack of recent practice made her intensely nervous. She drove through Seagate at twenty miles an hour and only speeded up when faced with a straight stretch of empty road.

'You're doing fine,' Justin said encouragingly.

Daring to glance at him, she saw that he was still

very pale and she knew he must be in pain. 'Where are we making for?' she asked. 'West City?'

Justin hesitated. 'It's a long way and means driving right into London, since there's no casualty department at St Andrews.'

'You mean you don't think you can stick it for so long?'

'I was wondering whether *you* could. Naturally I'd rather go to my own hospital.'

'Then that's where we'll go,' Paula said firmly. 'I don't mind about driving in London so much on a Sunday.'

In spite of her brave words she felt herself tensing up as the traffic increased. She was very glad indeed when the great bulk of West City loomed up before them. As she drew up near the big modern Accident Unit Justin put out his right hand and touched her fingers.

'You've been wonderful, Paula. I'm very grateful.'

It was on the tip of her tongue to tell him she didn't want his gratitude, that she would have been prepared to do much, much more for him than merely driving him to hospital if only he had wanted it that way.

Instead she merely said briefly, 'Perhaps I should say thank you to you for curing me of my phobia. I don't think I shall be so stupidly nervous about driving in future.'

'That's something achieved anyway.' He withdrew his hand and she heard him sigh. 'Otherwise it's been nothing but a disaster from beginning to end.'

Paula did not trust herself to comment. As she walked into West City with Justin at her side, she thought she had never felt so unreal in all her life. Sitting silently on one of the bright red chairs in the Accident Unit while he was being examined, it scarcely seemed possible that the day which had started with her impulsive leap onto the Seagate bus was ending like this.

'I'm afraid we'll have to admit Dr Stewart for a few days.'

She started violently as a youthful casualty officer addressed her suddenly. 'He really has broken his collar bone?'

'Oh yes, and he'll need time to get over the anaesthetic and recover from the shock.' He turned away and then remembered something. 'He wants to speak to you before you leave. The end cubicle.'

It would be about his car, she supposed. But when she drew the curtain back and looked in Justin made no reference to the car. He was sitting in a chair beside the examination couch, his face still desperately pale and his eyes strained.

'Of all the hellish things to happen!' He smiled wryly. 'You never know what Fate's got in store for you. But that wasn't what I wanted to say. Why were you going to Seagate, Paula?'

She had almost forgotten. Thinking back, she

recalled her intention to spend the day quietly planning the future, deciding whether or not to remain at Belton Park.

'I didn't really pick Seagate. I—I just wanted to go *somewhere* where I could be alone and—and make up my mind about something.'

'About what?' Justin demanded, his eyes on her face.

Paula hesitated and then chose the truth. 'Whether to leave the hospital and not bother about getting my SRN.'

'But it means so much to you!' He was obviously deeply shocked. 'And you've been doing so well too.'

'Have I?'

'Of course you have. You're an excellent nurse. You must be absolutely crazy even to suggest giving up. What on earth came over you?'

She could no longer meet his searching gaze and her eyes dropped to her clasped hands. 'I suppose I was a bit fed up with—everything.'

'Oh, Paula, my dear—' Justin's voice was warm and deep with emotion. 'I can't tell you how much it distresses me to think of you feeling like that. If only—' He broke off as a rattle of curtain rings heralded the entrance of a nurse.

'If you'll come this way, Dr Stewart.' She stood aside and waited for Paula to pass her.

'I'll take your car back to St Andrews for you, Justin.' She spoke over her shoulder as she prepared to leave. 'What shall I do with the keys?'

She could sense his hesitation and then he said quietly, 'Better hang on to them for a while. I shall know where they are when I want them but I'm afraid that won't be for some time.'

The small practical details had made her getaway simple. Without a backward glance Paula walked swiftly across the Accident Unit and outside. The drive to Belton Park occupied all her attention, giving no opportunity for thought, and it was not until she reached the haven of her room that she dared to let herself dwell on the events of that extraordinary day.

The tears came then, deluging her in a torrent of grief which left her exhausted and drained of all emotion so that she was no longer capable of making decisions of any kind. The problem of her future would have to wait until she felt more able to cope with it.

In the meantime she would just have to soldier on as best she could.

It never occurred to her that her mind might be made up for her.

CHAPTER THIRTEEN

'I'M going back to West City this afternoon,' Mary Shipton announced at lunch. 'And I can't say I'm sorry.' She glanced round the cramped dining room and then looked at Paula. 'Poor you—having to stay here for another seven or eight months.'

It was a strong desire to disagree with Mary which prompted Paula to protest.

'I've got quite fond of St Andrews so there's no need to feel sorry for me.'

Mary raised her eyebrows but made no further comment. She went off on the hospital mini-bus and Staff Nurse Coates, now fully recovered, took over. Bradshaw Ward immediately became a much pleasanter place in which to work.

They were just as busy and Sister Leyton still looked harassed but Paula no longer felt a sense of strain. Even Liz—whom they saw very frequently indeed because of Justin's enforced absence—seemed less critical and at times even quite human.

'I shall be glad when Dr Stewart gets back,' she said to Paula a few days after the accident. 'I never realised how much work he did until he wasn't here to do it.'

'I suppose he'll be away for quite a time?'

'Afraid so. He'll probably be discharged from

hospital tomorrow but after that he'll have sick leave. He's fixed up to go and stay with a relative somewhere on the south coast—lucky devil.'

Somehow Paula schooled her voice to ask the next question in a politely detached tone.

'I expect you've visited him. How is he getting on?'

'Okay—physically.' Liz frowned, her vivid blue eyes troubled. 'But he seemed so extraordinarily vague. I can't help wondering if he's still got a bit of concussion. I asked him about the accident but he couldn't really tell me much.'

She finished drying her hands after examining a patient and folded the towel neatly. 'And here's another puzzling thing. His car's back here—I've seen it myself—but he can't account for it being here. Don't you think that's strange?'

'Well—yes, I suppose so.' Paula looked away hastily.

'It's all locked up,' Liz went on, 'which means that somebody must have the keys.'

She sounded so bewildered that for one crazy moment Paula almost felt sorry for her. What on earth would she think if she knew that her fiancé's car keys were in the Nurses' Home, safely locked up in the box where Paula kept her most precious possessions?

The keys were her link with Justin, something which must inevitably bring him back to her, even if it was only for a moment.

She had formed the habit of taking them out and holding them in her hand every now and then, just because they were his. It was madness—she knew that—and yet strangely comforting.

The evening after her conversation with Liz she was sitting in her room with her textbooks spread out before her but she was making no attempt to do any work. With her future still undecided, it was harder than ever to concentrate on the duller aspects of nursing.

She was staring out of the window, her unseeing eyes fixed on a clump of early yellow chrysanthemums, when a tap on the door jerked her back to her surroundings.

'You're wanted on the phone.' A first-year nurse put her head in.

'Thanks.' Glad of the respite, Paula stood up and went along to the hooded telephone in an alcove off the hall. She said 'Hullo—Paula speaking' into the mouthpiece, half expecting to hear her mother's voice in reply.

But it was Justin.

'I'm so pleased to have caught you at the first attempt.' He sounded brisk and businesslike, and not at all as though he might be getting over concussion. 'I just had to speak to you before I left West City.'

'I can't think why,' she managed to say in a fair imitation of her normal tone.

'I shouldn't have thought it would be hard to

guess. It's that brief conversation we had on Sunday, just before they admitted me—I can't get it out of my mind. Paula, you mustn't even *think* about giving up nursing! You must be out of your mind even to contemplate it.'

The attack had taken her by surprise but she hastily rallied and fought back.

'I've probably been out of my mind about a lot of things but I can't see what it's got to do with you. Who gave you the right to ring me up and order me about?'

His reply came streaking back over the wires with the speed of an arrow. 'Nobody gave me the right but I can't help having opinions. You're not to throw away your whole career just because you happen to be feeling a bit fed up. Do you hear me?'

'I can hardly avoid it when you shout like that.'

'I'd do more than shout if I could get hold of you. I'd probably give you a good shaking—it's what you need,' he snapped.

'Then it's just as well you're not here, isn't it?' Paula was still clinging to the shreds of her own temper. 'And there's really no point in this conversation, Justin. Nobody's advice can possibly help me to make up my mind, least of all yours.'

There was silence at the other end and she could sense his change of mood even before he spoke.

'I suppose I asked for that,' he said quietly at last.

'I rather think you did.' She took a deep breath and hurried on. 'I'm going to ring off now. Liz says you're making a good recovery and I'm very glad to hear it. Goodbye.'

She hung up quickly, before he could say anything else, and went back to her room. The textbooks lay where she had left them and with an abrupt gesture she flung them into a heap on the floor.

She wouldn't be wanting them anymore. Justin had made up her mind for her—and not in the way which he had intended.

Pacing restlessly up and down the room, Paula made her plans. Miss Wallace was on holiday and nothing could be done until she returned. That meant another two weeks at least and so she might just as well finish her time on Bradshaw before giving in her notice.

Besides, she ought not to leave before Justin came back because of having to hand over his car keys.

Her mind settled, she felt strangely at peace. She wasn't happy, of course, but she was no longer in a state of inner turmoil.

The days began to slip by at lightning speed. Summer had ended and autumn was well established, and suddenly it was almost time to act on her decision.

But before she could do that, something happened.

'Come into the office a moment, please, Nurse Garland,' Sister ordered.

Slightly apprehensive in spite of a clear conscience, Paula obeyed.

'I've got a message for you, Nurse. Miss Grieves wants to see you at West City tomorrow afternoon at three o'clock.'

'Miss *Grieves*!' Paula stared at her in amazement. 'Whatever for?'

'She didn't take me into her confidence.' The thin anxious face was softened by a slight smile. 'So I'm afraid you'll have to wait to find out until you get there.'

Although time had been passing so swiftly, it seemed an age before Paula could set out for West City. She could not imagine why she had been sent for and every reason she thought up seemed more fantastic than the last. She was rigid with nervousness by the time she was summoned into the presence of the Principal Nursing Officer.

Last time she had been there gladioli brightened the austerity of the room. Now the vase on the desk contained bronze chrysanthemums. Otherwise nothing seemed changed.

'Sit down, Nurse.' Miss Grieves motioned her to a chair. 'I'm sure you must be wondering why I've sent for you so I'll come straight to the point. No doubt you think that in banishing you to Belton Park I removed you from my mind, but I can assure you that has not been the case at all.'

Unable to think of a suitable reply, Paula said nothing. She sat very still, her eyes on the calm face opposite.

'I'm glad to tell you that I have had extremely good reports from the two ward sisters with whom you have worked. Sister Knox gave you high praise, and Sister Leyton intends to do the same when you leave her for a medical ward.' She paused and smiled. 'Therefore, Nurse, I have come to the conclusion that I have been too hard on you in not letting you re-take your exam until next year.'

'I—I don't understand, Miss Grieves.'

Paula had spoken mechanically, her mind in a whirl. What about Miss Wallace? Surely *she* wouldn't have given her a good report? Or hadn't she even been asked? Maybe Miss Grieves considered the medical side of supreme importance, as indeed it was.

'Let me put it more plainly, Nurse,' the Principal Nursing Officer was saying. 'You may, if you wish, re-sit your finals in November instead of waiting until next May. I know that you did very well in the test at the end of your recent block study and I consider you have a good chance of passing.' Once more she paused. 'Well, Nurse? What do you think?'

Afterwards Paula had no idea what she had said. She remembered stammering confused thanks and babbling that she would try her hardest to justify Miss Grieves' confidence in her. And all the time at the back of her mind there was an overwhelming sense of gratitude because she hadn't spoilt it all in advance by handing in her notice.

She was still in a state of trance when she arrived back at St Andrews, and when she saw the taxi at the gate and Justin paying the driver she wondered for a moment if she was living a dream.

But Justin was real enough. Looking tanned and fit, he stood waiting for her, one arm still in a sling and the other outstretched in greeting.

'Paula! This is a bit of luck! I thought I might have to wait ages until you came off duty.'

'I'm free for the rest of the day,' she said simply, and then caught herself up with a gasp. She shouldn't be saying things like that to Justin!

'Super! Have you still got my car keys?'

'Of course I have.'

'Then what are we waiting for?'

Without a word Paula went to fetch the keys. But during the short walk she somehow managed to get a grip on herself and the trance-like state receded.

'Here you are, Justin.' She held them out to him but he did not take them.

'Sorry, love, but I'm still unable to drive.' He slipped his right arm into hers and turned her towards the car park. 'So if you wouldn't mind—'

'You mean you want me to drive you some-where?'

'I want you to drive *us*. I came here today special-ly to see you, so we could have that talk which got interrupted when I was knocked down.'

Paula's resistance stiffened. 'For goodness' sake—I can't think why you don't just give up. There's nothing more to be said—nothing.'

'I don't agree.' He thrust out his jaw and his grip on her arm tightened. 'You're damn well going to listen whether you want to or not. I know I went all wrong in the beginning. I invited you out and treated you like I was free to fall in love with you, and I didn't say a word about Liz in America. But I tried to explain long ago that at first it didn't seem to matter—'

Furiously she interrupted him. 'What's the good of repeating all that? You're engaged to Liz now and—'

'I am *not* engaged to Liz!' Justin shouted.

She stared at him blankly. 'Not?'

'Liz is engaged to a doctor in America. They fell in love practically at first sight but she refused to make it a definite engagement until she'd cleared herself with me. She and I never had even a vague sort of understanding but we did believe ourselves to be in love for a short time. I guess I was dazzled by her looks to begin with but I soon learned to like her very much.'

They had reached the car. Automatically, her brain reeling, Paula unlocked it and they got in.

'Oh, Paula darling—what I felt for Liz bears no resemblance to the feeling I have for you.' Justin took her limp hand in his. 'I *love* you, deeply and truly and honestly. I know I've made an awful mess of things but do you think you could possibly forgive me and let us start afresh?'

She scarcely seemed to have heard his question. She was gazing at him with her heart in her eyes but he was too distressed to notice.

'Did you say you loved me, Justin? I just can't seem to believe it somehow. I thought you were going to marry Liz and I was so unhappy, but now everything has changed and I think I'm afraid there may be some mistake.'

'*You* were unhappy?' he exclaimed. 'I thought I'd made you angry and scornful. It never occurred to me that you might be miserable as well as me. Oh, Paula, what a fool I've been! You've got an awful lot to forgive me for but for God's sake don't tell me you can't manage it.'

'Don't let's talk about forgiveness,' she urged. 'I expect I behaved pretty badly too. I was intolerant and I wouldn't listen when you tried to talk to me. Let's put the past completely behind us.'

'I'm only too willing, darling,' Justin said tenderly. 'But there's one thing I've got to know. Could you possibly love me, just a little?'

There was no hesitation about Paula's reply. Her eyes were shining with sincerity and a hint of tears.

'I love you a very great deal but I never thought I would have the chance to tell you. I can still hardly believe—'

He did not wait for her to finish the sentence. His

right arm came round her with a hungry need as great as her own. They clung together with a sort of desperation, obliterating the past with the sweetness of the present, finding in each other's nearness a happiness so intense that neither wanted the embrace ever to end.

At last Paula opened her eyes and looked round at the inside of the little car. 'Were we going some place?'

'It doesn't seem to have been necessary.' Justin smiled and kissed her eyes, her nose, her throat. 'When will you marry me, darling?'

'When I've got my SRN,' she told him promptly.

'Not till then?' He was incredulous. 'But that won't be until *next year*.'

'With any luck it'll be sooner than that.' Happily, she told about the interview with Miss Grieves. 'What with one thing and another, love, this has been the most wonderful day in my whole life.'

There was another a few weeks later when the exam results came out and Paula found she was now entitled to call herself Nurse Garland, SRN. But the happiest and most wonderful day of all was the one on which she married Justin.

Doctor Nurse Romances

Romance in modern medical life

Read more about the lives and loves of doctors and nurses in the fascinatingly different backgrounds of contemporary medicine. These are the three Doctor Nurse romances to look out for next month.

LEGACY OF LOVE
Hazel Fisher

NEW CALEDONIAN NURSE
Lilian Darcy

THE MAGIC OF LIVING
Betty Neels

Buy them from your usual paperback stockist, or write to: Mills & Boon Reader Service, P.O. Box 236, Thornton Rd, Croydon, Surrey CR9 3RU, England. Readers in South Africa-write to: Mills & Boon Reader Service of Southern Africa, Private Bag X3010, Randburg, 2125.

Mills & Boon
the rose of romance

 **ROMANCE**

Variety is the spice of romance

Each month, Mills & Boon publish new romances. New stories about people falling in love. A world of variety in romance – from the best writers in the romantic world. Choose from these titles in September.

THE DARK ONE Vanessa James
CARVER'S BRIDE Nicola West
PRELUDE TO A SONG Margaret Pargeter
ISLAND OF THE DAWN Penny Jordan
SEASON OF MISTS Anne Mather
THE SILVER VEIL Margaret Way
HOUSE OF MIRRORS Yvonne Whittal
ALL ELSE CONFUSION Betty Neels
SECOND BEST WIFE Rachel Lindsay
FORBIDDEN SURRENDER Carole Mortimer
THE WOLF MAN Sandra Clark
CAST A TENDER SHADOW Isabel Dix

On sale where you buy paperbacks. If you require further information or have any difficulty obtaining them, write to: Mills & Boon Reader Service, PO Box 236, Thornton Road, Croydon, Surrey CR9 3RU, England.

Mills & Boon
the rose of romance

Accept FOUR BEST-SELLING ROMANCES FREE

You have nothing to lose – and a whole new world of romance to gain. Send this coupon today, and enjoy the novels that have already enthralled thousands of readers!

✂ -